Make It Real

Also by

Chris Walters

The Tashaverse:
No One Like You
Make It Real
Send Me An Angel

Goddess Good

Visit the link above to listen to the Make It Real
soundtrack on Spotify.

To everyone brave enough to ask for help, and to everyone kind enough to give it.

Content Warnings:

Brief allusions to poor parenting. (not depicted)
Brief allusions to domestic violence. (not depicted)
Brief allusions to alcohol and drug abuse. (not depicted)
Open door descriptions of intimacy.

Contents

Chapter 1

Oh, Pretty Woman

Roy Orbison

Where did my pen go? I swear it was right there a minute ago.

Finding both the writing implement and the culprit didn't take long. Quincy Rogers located Dolly Purrton under the couch where she had chased his pen, the cat hunched territorially over her prize. She smacked at his hand as he attempted to retrieve his pen.

"Okay, okay...I'll use a different one."

Defeated, Quincy returned to his desk in the corner, where he returned to work. He started working from home during the pandemic and kept doing so after the all-clear was given. Working on the backend of websites was a job that lent itself well to work-from-home. Being around all day enabled him to take better care of his daughter, Ruby. The year of the pandemic, which mandated distance learning, was challenging for both parent and child, but they managed to get through it. They were happier once Ruby attended school in person again. Quincy liked seeing her off to school every day and meeting her to walk home in the afternoon.

What concerned Quincy this particular day wasn't his workload but the company's latest escalation in its continuing efforts to bring workers back to the office. So far, Quincy had been able to avoid these demands, but he feared his ability to continue to do so would soon come to an end. He dreaded the idea of returning to the office. Quincy felt fewer distractions at home, and his metrics showed he was far more productive. Unfortunately, evidence and sound reasoning were useless against the uncaring demands of corporate dogma. Quincy knew he would eventually lose this battle, making him miserable.

Later, he took a short break to walk Ruby home from school. Dolly Purrton greeted Quincy and Ruby with adorable little cat cries and purrs when they returned, providing Quincy a brief moment to rescue his pen while the cat rolled around. Pen in hand, Quincy watched Dolly Purrton's antics. The white fur underneath the black made rippling stripes as she twisted and rolled. He smiled, thinking how lucky he was to find such an unusually marked cat at the shelter.

Quincy happily spent a few minutes asking Ruby how her classes were, what she ate for lunch, whether she had fun during recess, and all the other questions that made him feel part of her day. Raising a child on his own was a lot of work, but Ruby was worth it.

After work, Quincy coaxed Ruby into donning her coat and then got himself ready before walking back to school for the first PTA meeting of the calendar year. As a young, single father, PTA meetings were a bit of a minefield. Well-meaning parents always had a seemingly endless supply of single friends, cousins, or sisters who would be "just perfect" for him. Quincy learned to be wary of these offers, although every once in a while, his ability to deflect and demure failed, and he ended up on a blind date. Those generally went poorly, but he did sometimes at least get to commiserate with a kindred soul who was just as embarrassed to be there as he was. This particular PTA had the potential for disaster written all over it because Rachel would almost certainly be there. He strongly considered skipping it; however, his sense of duty won out. Quincy was filled with both dread and hope at the prospect of seeing Rachel again. They had started dating in September and really clicked. Their dates were fun; they had amazing conversations and then, eventually, really good sex. Quincy had been considering the next steps when everything came to a crashing halt right before Christmas. Rachel and her estranged husband decided to give their marriage a second chance, and suddenly, Quincy was single again.

There were about twenty parents in attendance at tonight's PTA meeting, including Rachel and...Simon? Steve? Something starting with 'S.' Quincy tried not to look at Rachel, but he couldn't help himself. She looked alluring, and he couldn't help but remember what she looked like underneath her modest attire. Rachel was also holding hands with her husband, which caused Quincy a pang of guilt.

Are they holding hands because they are back in love? Maybe they are just trying hard to fake it until they make it. I have to stop thinking about her. She's moved on...moved back...whatever. She's done with me and back with him, and I'm not going to be a homewrecker. Oh damn, I thought our sex was good, but maybe I was so bad that she decided she would be better off trying to get back with her husband. Nope. Can't think that way. I swear, from here on out, I will never date anyone who hasn't signed divorce papers.

Quincy tried to focus on what Sharon, the PTA president, said. Something about the Spring Fair fundraiser: she was looking for volunteers to plan and organize the fundraiser. Mary already volunteered because, of course, she did. Mary's energy was legendary. She was also constantly trying to find him the right woman. Despite the endless matchmaking, she was genuinely lovely, and they got along well. Getting along with Mary was good because she volunteered for everything. Quincy raised his hand to volunteer for the Spring Fair and heard Mary's unabashed squee of delight. Out of the corner of his eye, Quincy saw Rachel glance at him, but she quickly turned back to her husband and did not raise her hand to volunteer.

There was a rustling behind Quincy, and he saw Sharon point past him, asking, "Thank you, and you are?"

"I'm Tasha..." He chuckled nervously. "This is my first time here. Hi, everyone."

Quincy craned his neck around just in time to see a tall, beautiful woman wave shyly at the group. Reflexively, his eyes drifted to her caramel-toned left hand and noted the absence of a ring on the third finger.

You just got dumped a month ago by someone in this room. Do not get the reputation of the guy who slept his way through every single mother in the PTA. Although, she would be worth it. Wow.

"Uh, hi. I'm Quincy, and I'm looking forward to working with you," he whispered.

"Thanks, and good to meet you. I'm Tasha...which I just said."

Quincy returned to facing forward, which his back greatly appreciated. He tried to focus on the rest of the meeting and not think too much about the ex-girlfriend across the aisle or the stunning stranger behind him.

Once the meeting was over, Mary rushed over to corral Quincy and Tasha, setting up a meeting at a local coffee house on Saturday afternoon, when they all agreed on the time and place that worked. Mary also set up a text group, saving Quincy the effort of finding an excuse to acquire Tasha's number, and then rushed off to talk to someone else, leaving Quincy and Tasha standing awkwardly together.

"So...first time at a PTA meeting, huh?"

Brilliant opening, Quincy. Cyrano, you are not.

"Yeah, I wasn't entirely sure what to expect. Not gonna lie, though, I did predict there would be gluten-free, nut-free, vegan cookies, and I wasn't wrong."

"It's Portland, that's just expected."

"It definitely is."

Tasha's laugh gave Quincy heart palpitations. As far as jokes went, his was flimsy and obvious, but he was thankful it elicited some kind of laugh. He briefly considered trying to follow it up with a pun but decided not to press his luck. Instead, he asked, "Which grade is your kid in?"

"Third, but technically not my kid."

I'm about to blow this. I know it.

"Your younger sibling, then?"

Tasha laughed. "You're funny and cute, too—"

Yes! She thinks I'm cute.

"—but Sophia is my partner's daughter."

Partner. Well, that ends that. At least I'm funny and cute. If I'm lucky, maybe she has a sister. For once, I wouldn't mind being set up.

"Huh, Sophia. The name sounds familiar. My daughter, Ruby, is also in the third grade."

"Ruby, of course. Sophia told me about her. Hang on...sandy blonde hair with a Barbie backpack?"

"Yes, that's her. How—"

"I thought you looked familiar." Tasha's smile could light a skyscraper. "I've been walking Sophia to and from school every day, so I've seen them together a few times. Ruby seems like a really nice kid."

"She is. Speaking of, we should probably be heading home. Would you like to meet her officially?"

"Of course, I brought Sophia with me so you can meet her. Maybe we can arrange a playdate sometime?" Tasha lowered her voice conspiratorially. "That's a thing parents do, right? Sorry, I'm uncomfortably new to this whole parenting thing."

"No worries, and yes, a playdate sounds fun—provided the girls are interested, of course."

"Does Ruby roller skate?"

"Yes, she loves it, but I feel bad because I don't often have time to take her. I think skating would be a great playdate."

"Does your partner not take Ruby, or..."

"No partner. Single dad."

"Oh, I'm sorry. I shouldn't have asked."

"Tasha, it's totally fine, especially since you are new to the whole parenting thing. Hang around the PTA, and you will quickly learn *everything* about *everyone*. Trust me."

They reached the childcare area and were introduced to their respective children.

"So, you and Sophia's father are married then?"

Tasha laughed, tried to speak, then laughed some more, finally getting control of herself after Sophia tugged at her sleeve. Quincy felt the heat in his cheeks as he blushed.

Wow, I'm not sure exactly what I said, but I must have screwed up badly.

"Sorry." Tasha let out one more giggle before continuing, "Let's just say that my relationship with Sophia's father is rocky at best. On the other hand, Sophia's mother is the love of my life, and we are working on the marriage thing."

"I'm really sorry. I shouldn't have assumed—"

"Quincy, you're fine. We each asked a very embarrassing question about the other's personal life, so let's call it even. I'll text about a playdate, and maybe you can meet Megan sometime."

"Megan is..."

"Sophia's mom and my girlfriend slash fiancée."

"That would be great. Both the playdate and meeting up with you and Megan."

Chapter 2

Bartender

Lady A

There is an art to bartending. It's not just about making great drinks, although mixology is obviously an essential part of it. A great bartender provided people with the experience they needed, not just the drink they wanted. At work, Mandana Davani was the eye of the hurricane, smoothly moving from patron to patron, keeping the drink orders for the wait staff flowing, and keeping the cooks from knifing each other. Her regulars loved her—Javier, who was always sitting at the end of the bar and currently reading the new Lavender LeFleur bestseller—and liked a dirty martini with no extra chatter. Becca, often found slowly sipping a mojito after her shift at the hospital, preferred her drinks light and gossip lighter. Sometimes, Becca also required a hand fending off overly amorous suitors. Mandana knew her regulars but was just as good with new guests because any new guest could soon be a regular.

Mandana quit school halfway through her MBA to focus on bartending. She had been near the top of her class, but big business never called to her. Bartending, though, that's what she loved. Mandana made a small fortune slinging drinks in New York, Miami, Vegas, and LA, but none of those places felt like home to her. Her car broke down in Portland after she came back from skiing in British Columbia, and she liked the city so much that she moved there as soon as her lease was up.

Mandana had Tuesdays and Wednesdays off, so she was practicing yoga at her neighborhood studio this particular Tuesday. After class, she chatted with Megan, the new instructor who had taken over this time slot a month ago.

"Hey, Mandana, how did today feel for you?"

"Really good, thank you. I want to say how much I appreciate your teaching style. Having your quiet guidance is so much better than someone telling me I'm doing it wrong from across the room. You foster a comfortable environment."

"Aw, thank you. I'm grateful to hear your impression." Megan grinned. "Not that you ever need correction. I saw you in my Saturday morning class, too. It's great to see you twice a week."

"I will admit, I debated going to the Saturday morning class. I'm a bartender, so as you might imagine, I am up late on Friday nights. Getting up to take your class was a struggle, but I'm so glad I did."

"Good thing I have the mid-morning class and not the early time slot, then." Megan gave her an inquisitive look. "Bartending sounds fascinating. You must have so many stories."

"Too many to count. What about you? How long have you been teaching yoga?"

"Almost ten years now, off and on. Teaching yoga isn't my main job, though. Currently, I'm a substitute teacher for Portland Public, but I'll be going permanent as soon as possible. What about you?"

"I started bartending in college and did it full-time once I dropped out of grad school."

"You dropped out of grad school to tend bar? I feel like there's a story there."

"Want to grab a bite, and I can tell you all about it?"

The other woman blushed before stammering out, "I dunno, I should probably get home to my daughter and girlfriend."

Mandana giggled. "I'm sorry, Megan. I wasn't asking you out." She raised her eyebrows lecherously. "I mean, don't get me wrong, you are super hot, but I haven't been with a woman for quite a long time. I really think we could be friends, though."

Megan blushed again. "I'm sorry I misread you. Yes, absolutely. Let me text Tasha."

"If you want, maybe Tasha and your daughter could join us."

"That's a great idea. They should be done with the PTA meeting by now. Hang on...Tasha says she's in. Where should we meet them?"

"Does the little pub around the corner work for you?"

"I've never been there, but maybe Tasha has. So long as Sophia can get something, then we should be okay."

"Great, let me grab my things, and I'll see you out front."

"See you soon."

Mandana didn't have to wait long before she spotted Megan walking toward the door with her water bottle and yoga mat in hand. She was looking forward to getting to know Megan better and meeting Megan's girlfriend. Mandana got along well with the people she worked with, but she didn't have anyone she would call a friend in her life.

My lifestyle for the last dozen or so years has not really lent itself to forming friendships or really any other close bonds, she thought. *Roaming from city to city, surrounded by shallow and narcissistic people, and working in a high turnover job, there weren't many people worth trying to get close with. Trying to settle down in a new city, I'm realizing just how big of a hole that is in my life. I would actually like to make friends, maybe even find a boyfriend at some point. Megan seems genuinely friendly and down-to-earth, and hopefully, we will get along.*

The two women met again on the sidewalk and chatted about the yoga class as they walked to the pub.

"Does this place look all right to you?"

"Oh, yeah. They have a kid's menu, so Sophia should be fine. Are you sure you want to go to a pub? You know, being a bartender and all."

"*Totally*. I love a good pub. Thank you for checking, though. Want to wait at the bar?"

"Sounds good."

They grabbed stools at the bar and got beers.

Mandana eyed Megan. "I love your hair."

"Oh, thank you. The purple was Tasha's suggestion. I dyed my hair blond for my ex-husband, but no one liked it. Tasha suggested I try something different. I like having purple hair, but I don't love it. I want to return to my natural hair once it grows out again."

"I see the red layer underneath. That's a beautiful color," Mandana gushed. "Why did you ever go blond?"

"If I had a nickel for every time someone asked me that...I guess things with Brad had gotten a bit stale, so I thought blond would be more attractive to him. Turns out I should have gone brunette."

"Why brunette?"

"Because the woman he was banging on the side was brunette." Megan chuckled ruefully.

"Wow, I'm sorry. I didn't mean to bring up bad memories—"

Megan casually waved off Mandana's apology. "Don't worry about it. I was distraught, especially since I walked in on them, you know...*in flagrante delicto*. Anyway, leaving my homewrecking shitweasel of an ex-husband brought Tasha back into my life, and I couldn't be happier."

"Back into your life? How did you know Tasha?"

"We were roommates in college. She was my maid of honor and is Sophia's godmother. I guess somewhere along the way, we just got sucked into our own lives. When I left my ex, I didn't know where to go. I called Tasha, and she let me and Sophia crash with her. It was *amazing*, Mandana. We reconnected immediately. All those bonds were still there—just a bit rusty. Suddenly, we were best friends again, and then somewhere along the way, we realized we were much more than friends. Now I'm divorced, in love with my best friend, and soon to be married—this time for good."

I wish I had friends like that. Maybe some of my high school friends, but it's been fifteen years since I've seen or heard from most of them. Listening to Megan makes me realize just how lonely I've been.

Putting her newfound heartache aside, Mandana exclaimed, "That's amazing. I'm glad it worked out for you in the end. If you could go back to college, would you have done anything differently?"

"Yes and no. I don't ever regret Sophia. I do regret some other choices. I shouldn't have stayed with my ex as long as I did. As you might imagine, we are not in a great place right now, but hopefully getting better. He realizes Tasha and I love each other and is working on being less of an asshole. Having Sophia means I can't ever be truly done with him, but I did at least get rid of the blond hair."

They both laughed at her last remark. Mandana tried to return the conversation to a lighter topic by querying, "Are you going to keep coloring your hair your natural shade, or are you going all natural?"

"I'm still thinking about it. What about you?"

"I started dying my hair when I got more gray hairs than I could pluck. I guess sometime in my mid-twenties. After I turned thirty, I stopped. I'm lucky I don't have a lot of grays so far, but I've decided I'm not going to fight getting older."

"Well, it's working for you. Your salt-and-pepper with the start of silver wings at the temples is *gorgeous*." Megan paused as if seeing Mandana anew. "Actually, you are flat-out gorgeous all over."

Mandana chuckled. "Megan, are you coming on to me?"

She looked panicked. "No, I—"

"I'm teasing you." Mandana saw a tall, stunningly beautiful African American woman walk in with a red-headed child who looked much like Megan. "Oh, *wow*. Speaking of gorgeous, is she your girlfriend?"

Megan spun around, made a squee noise, and practically sprinted over to the woman, giving her a big hug and a passionate kiss.

I'll take that as a 'Yes.'

Mandana strolled up to the trio. "Hi, you must be Sophia and Tasha. I'm Mandana."

"Good to meet you, Mandana. You're in Megan's yoga class?"

"Yes, she is a great teacher. I'm still new to Portland, so I'm hoping to make new friends."

Tasha smiled fondly at Megan, who was busy talking with Sophia. "I get that. Megan is new to Portland, too. We were roommates all four years in college, and even before we got to the university, Megan called me up to introduce herself, and I immediately knew we'd become friends. She really is the best."

The indisputable love on Tasha's face melted Mandana's heart. *There's a life goal for me. Find someone who looks at me the way Tasha looks at Megan. Oh, wow, and the way Megan looks at Tasha. They're in love, for sure.*

Mandana took this opportunity to get them a table where the family joined her.

Megan introduced Mandana to Sophia, who gushed, "Your tattoos are so pretty!"

"Thank you, Sophia." Mandana pushed her short sleeves up to her shoulders to completely expose the full-sleeve tattoo on her left arm as well as the tattoos on her upper right arm.

"Your tattoos are stunningly beautiful," Tasha concurred. "Do you have more?"

"I do, on my upper back. You?"

Tasha pulled her sleeves up, showing off her tattoos. "I have one on my thigh as well."

"Oh, I like the cat paw prints. Do you have a cat?"

"We have two."

"I like cats but don't have any right now. Megan, what about you? Any tattoos?"

Megan blushed. "No, although looking at both of you, I'm starting to feel like I should get some. I'm not sure what I would get, though. Did the sleeve hurt?" Megan pointed at the full sleeve on Mandana's left arm.

"Oh, yeah," Mandana laughed. "It was *excruciating* but totally worth it."

"It really is gorgeous; can I ask what it is?"

"The woman on the throne is Mandana, princess of Media and mother of Cyrus the Great. She is the first of the great Persian queens and obviously my namesake. The iconography around her is from ancient Persia. Further down, you can see the winged lion, which is another ancient Persian symbol."

"Wow, um, I suddenly feel so plain."

"Aw, you are definitely not plain, my love." Tasha gently consoled Megan. "You seem very in touch with your heritage, Mandana. That's really awesome."

"I agree with Tasha and Megan. You aren't plain at all." Mandana winked at Tasha. "Give Tasha and me some time, and we'll come up with some good ideas for you. No tramp stamps, though."

The three adults laughed.

After they ate, Mandana looked at Megan and said, "You wanted to know why I dropped out of school to tend bar, right?"

"Yeah."

"My parents are both very driven and very successful, but neither of them actually enjoys what they do. I feel their lives aren't as fulfilling as they could be because of that. They pushed me toward business, and I'm very good at it—I was near the top of my class in the MBA program—but I wouldn't say I liked it. When I turned twenty-one, I started moonlighting as a bartender and loved it. I liked the people, the atmosphere, and the power."

"The power?"

"A good bartender can be like...a quarterback, controlling the pace and the vibe and keeping everything flowing. Literally and figuratively."

"Mom, like a pivot," Sophia interjected.

Mandana was curious. "A pivot?"

Megan chuckled. "It's a roller derby term. They are the pack leaders in that sport."

"I've heard of roller derby but haven't ever seen it."

"It's a lot of fun. Tasha introduced us to it. Sophia is going to try out for the Rose City Rollers' Rose Petals. The Petals are their seven to twelve juniors' program."

Mandana looked at Sophia, who was practically bouncing with excitement. "I guess I need to go see some roller derby." Mandana grinned at Sophia, who grinned back. "Back to my story. I loved bartending and saw the MBA as just a road to the life my parents had. I decided I didn't want to be like my parents, so I dropped out. My education hasn't gone to waste, though. I worked at high-end places in New York, then moved around some. Working in posh places where hedge fund bros and oil princes drop obscene amounts of money meant a shitload of tips for me, and I have invested wisely."

"How do your parents feel about your decision?" "Oh, they *hate* it, but I don't care. I love what I do, and I'm very good at it."

"I'm very happy for you, and thank you for not asking me out—" Megan snickered before continuing, "—to tell me about it. Now, though, we need to get this little angel home. We both have school in the morning. Will I see you again on Saturday?"

"Definitely. Tasha, will you be coming?"

Megan and Tasha looked at each other, giggling at a private, unspoken joke. "Maybe. This has been fun. It was wonderful to meet you, Mandana."

"You too, Tasha. And it was charming to meet you, Sophia. I would love to hear more about roller derby."

They exchanged a few more goodbyes before they all left. Mandana felt great about how the evening went. She hoped it would be the first step toward a new friendship.

Chapter 3

One Night Love Affair

Bryan Adams

The rest of the week dragged on interminably for Quincy. Work projects kept him busy but unfulfilled. Most of his time was spent fixing problems caused by mismatched software. He was sure management acquired new software, blithely assuming it would work seamlessly with the medley of the existing software, even though that was never the case. Instead of doing the creative tasks he enjoyed, Quincy seemed to spend more and more time slogging through Frankencode to duct tape software together enough to keep things running. With the impending return to the office edict looming, he wasn't sure how much more he could take.

Quincy wasn't looking forward to his Saturday planning meeting with Mary and Tasha, but at least it wouldn't involve being neck-deep in code. The three exchanged text messages to determine where to meet, deciding on a local coffee shop. Just an hour before their meeting, Quincy received the unpleasant news that his babysitter for Ruby fell through. He texted Mary and Tasha about this issue and said he was seeking a solution. Tasha texted back immediately, suggesting he bring Ruby to her place, where her girlfriend would watch her and Sophia. Quincy immediately agreed and asked for the address.

"Hey, kiddo. Change of plans. We're going to go over to Sophia's place, and her mom will watch the two of you while I have my meeting."

"I thought I was staying here."

"I'm sorry. The babysitter couldn't make it. On the plus side, you get to hang out with Sophia. I seem to recall you saying she was nice."

"She is. Can't I just stay here, though? I am only going to read my book anyway. I'll be good."

"I know you would be good, but it's...complicated. I trust you, but I still get worried about what could happen. Please do this for me because it makes me feel better knowing an adult is watching you. You're my whole world, Ruby, and I want to keep you safe."

"Okay, Daddy. I love you, too."

"Pack your book and anything else you want to take. We'll leave in about ten minutes."

Quincy was thankful Ruby was a generally good kid. Single parenting was tough on the best days, but having a child who was happy to have her nose in a book was helpful. Quincy had heard plenty of horror stories from other parents. Rachel's two boys apparently loved wrestling all over the house.

I definitely need to stop thinking of her.

Tasha didn't live far away, so the drive over was quick. If it hadn't been January, then they would have walked. He texted Tasha to let her know they were there, and she came down to open the building door for them. They walked back to her apartment, where she introduced Quincy to two attractive women in yoga attire.

"Quincy and Ruby, this is my girlfriend, Megan. And this is our friend, Mandana. Megan teaches yoga a couple of times a week, which is where she met Mandana."

"Hello, it's great to meet you both." Quincy was trying hard not to stare. He didn't want to seem creepy, but he didn't want to seem rude by ignoring them, either.

"Fiancée, actually. However, we haven't made it official with rings or anything. Good to meet you and Ruby."

Mandana looked surprised. "What? You didn't mention that you two were engaged. I'm not surprised, though. Quincy, Ruby, it's very nice to meet you as well. Megan and I were going to have some tea. I hope you don't mind me being here."

"Oh, no. That's perfectly fine, Mandana. I'm very grateful Megan could watch Ruby on such short notice."

"It's my pleasure. You and Ruby aren't allergic to cats, are you?"

"No, we have a cat ourselves. Ah, I'm guessing these are the cats in question."

Tasha introduced the cats. "The black one is Nocturne, and the orange one is Julius. Y'all are the first new people Julius has met since we got him. I had Nocturne before Megan and Sophia moved in. Sophia thought she might get lonely during the day, so we got Julius to keep Nocturne company."

"Aw, she's very thoughtful. I work from home, at least for now, so I keep Dolly Purrton company."

Mandana cackled. "Dolly Purrton? That's awesome. I'm guessing your wife's name isn't Jolene, then."

"No wife. I'm raising Ruby on my own."

"Wow, I'm so sorry. I shouldn't have assumed."

"From what I've heard, Quincy here is quite the catch. Mary, the other person we are meeting with today, has been singing his praises to me. Unfortunately for Quincy, I'm already taken." Tasha grinned and gave Megan a hip bump. "But luckily for Quincy, Mary has an extensive list of other single women for him to meet."

"Really now?" Mandana looked amused.

"Ugh, don't remind me." Quincy buried his face in his hands. "Mary is relentless. She said I am, and I quote, 'a unicorn.' Supposedly, that's a good thing. At least when I was dating Rachel, Mary left me alone."

"Rachel, Rachel. You don't mean the one at the PTA meeting, do you?"

"Yeah. That one.""Wasn't she there with–"

"Her husband? They were separated, but now they are trying to reconcile. I swear I didn't date her while they were together."

Tasha put her arm around Megan, saying, "I'm glad to hear you aren't a homewrecker. Her going back to her husband must have been tough, though."

"Eh, it's been hard, especially seeing them together at the PTA meeting. That was the first time I saw her since the breakup. On the plus side, it's much easier on the ego knowing she broke up with me to get back together with her husband. It's a lot harder having someone break up with me because I already have a kid. But ever since Rachel broke things off, Mary has told me about her cousin who is in town and very single."

"I can help you. Give me your phone." Mandana walked over to him with her hand out.

Quincy wasn't sure what was happening, but he handed her the phone anyway. He was pleasantly surprised when she wrapped her arm around him and held the phone for a selfie. Quincy was shocked when Mandana kissed him on the cheek as she took the selfie.

"There you go. Now you can tell Mary you have a girlfriend." She handed Quincy his phone.

"Wow, thanks." His cheeks were burning, partially from blushing and partially because he could still feel the lingering heat from Mandana's kiss. "You didn't have to."

"I know, but it's fun. Plus, you seem like a nice guy, so I'm happy to be your fake girlfriend for five seconds to keep you safe from Mary's cousin. Although, what if her cousin is hot and very ready to mingle if you know what I mean?"

Quincy felt his cheeks burning even hotter. "Experience suggests that isn't the case. Plus, I doubt she is more beautiful than you."

"Mmm, don't you have a silver tongue? Tasha, your friend here, knows how to compliment a girl. Since you're such a charmer, let me make sure your other cheek doesn't feel lonely—" Quincy held his breath as Mandana leaned in for a quick kiss on his other cheek. "—now, don't you two have a meeting to go to?"

"We do. Let's hit the road, Quincy. Love, I will see you in a bit. Mandana, it was good seeing you again. Kids, have fun." Tasha snagged Quincy's elbow, dragging him in her wake.

They were all the way down the block before Quincy's mind finally caught up to his body. He shook his head, trying to sort his thoughts out. "Is she always like that?"

"Who? Mandana? Honestly, I'm not sure. This morning was just the third time I met her. Megan knows her a bit better. We got dressed up for date night last night and went to the place where Mandana is the bartender. It was a fun evening, and we chatted with her when there was a lull. If it makes you feel better, she is extraordinarily good at taking care of people. I suspect you aren't the first person she has helped with a fake dating photo."

Why does the idea of her taking other fake photos disturb me? I just met her, and I'm being stupid.

Quincy shook his head and sighed. "She seems nice."

Tasha cocked an eyebrow. "Yes, she does. Are you interested?"

"Um, maybe? I don't know. I had a really good thing going on with Rachel, and then it ended so abruptly. I honestly don't know where my head is these days. We were only together for about four months, but I was starting to think maybe it might last for a long time, and then suddenly it's over, and I'm alone again."

"I'm sorry, I didn't know. That sounds very rough. Was Rachel the first woman you felt serious about since..."

"Since Ruby's mom? We were never married and hadn't planned on getting married. We were young and stupid, but then Ruby came along, and suddenly, I was raising an infant on my own. Dating has been a challenge ever since. Rachel was the first woman I seriously considered long-term."

"Oof. I can see why you feel like you don't know where your head is."

"Yeah. Maybe I should just go out with Mary's cousin. What's the worst that could happen?"

Tasha semi-seriously responded, "Just what every girl wants to hear."

"I mean...I will try my best to show her a good time."

Tasha waggled her eyebrows suggestively. "Oh, I bet you will."

Quincy laughed, "Okay, let's not get ahead of ourselves here. It's a date with Mary's cousin, and I haven't even said 'yes' yet."

"*Yet.* There's the shop, and there's Mary. You can give her the good news in person."

"You're killing me, Tasha."

Their meeting was productive. Mary was a fountain of ideas, while Quincy and Tasha approached it from a more practical project management perspective. The two of them were able to sift through Mary's stream of consciousness to extract workable ideas to potentially implement and lay down a framework for making the event happen. All three felt very good about their progress when they wrapped up.

Quincy was tempted to use the photo of his new fake girlfriend to deflect Mary but instead agreed to go out with her cousin. He was decidedly leery of another blind date but needed to move on from Rachel. Quincy didn't think this Sara person would be 'The One,' but a date with her could be a start. He was taken aback when Mary suggested that evening for a first date. Quincy said he would think about it.

As he and Tasha walked back to her place so he could collect Ruby, she offered, "If you want, Megan and I can watch Ruby tonight so you can go out with Sara. You know, only if you want to go out on a blind date."

"I'm not sure I really want to go out on a blind date, but maybe it will be good for me. Help me stop thinking about Rachel."

Tasha shrugged. "Up to you."

Quincy sighed. "I think I'm going to do it."

"Speaking of doing it, if you get lucky, just text me, and we can watch Ruby overnight."

"*Thanks?*" He said with a dubious tone, adding, "I doubt I'll end up in bed on a first date."

"You never know. You're kinda hot. Do you have any sexy clothes, or is it all dad wear?"

"Thanks? I feel like I have some sexy outfits. Maybe?" Quincy felt suddenly nervous.

"Well, you've got the hot nerd look going already. I guess the question is, do you want to lean into that or dial it back?"

"Lean into it, I think. It's been over a month since Rachel, and, uh...never mind."

"You've got an itch to scratch? Lemme call someone." Tasha whipped out her phone. "Hi, Maria."

...

"I've got a friend, and he wants to look good for a first date. Do you know anyone?"

...

"Cool, thanks."

...

"Megan and I are great. Yes, we will absolutely be there for your Valentine's bash. This will be so much fun to go to with my fiancée."

...

"Okay, thanks. Bye." Tasha hung up. "My friend knows a guy who can help you out. I'll text you the details. You don't have to if you don't want to. I won't judge."

"Thank you, that's very nice. I will check him out."

"We can watch Ruby longer this afternoon if you want to go now."

Quincy stopped in his tracks, stunned by Tasha's kindness. "Really? You don't mind?"

Her lips curled into a playful grin. "Well, let's make sure the girls are getting along first. If they are having a good time, then you can go get sexified and have your blind date with Mary's cousin, Sara."

"Good thinking."

"I even have a restaurant recommendation for you."

Later that evening, Quincy found himself at an upscale bar and grill, waiting for Sara to arrive. Feeling the need for some liquid courage, he sidled up to the bar. As Quincy checked the entrance, he heard a semi-familiar voice behind him say, "Quincy, right?" He turned around to see Mandana looking at him from behind the bar.

"Oh, hi. *Mandy?*" Quincy noted her nametag.

"Of all the gin joints, in all the towns, in all the world, he walks into mine."

Quincy laughed, "Casablanca?"

"*Oh,*" Mandana purred. "A cultured man, I see. Yes, I go by Mandy sometimes. It's easier for people to pronounce. What are you doing here?"

"I—" Quincy chuckled to cover the butterflies in his stomach. "—decided to go on a blind date with Mary's cousin after all."

"Brave man. Is that why you got all dressed up?"

"Yeah, although I feel weird. I've never worn a shirt this tight before."

He watched as Mandana gave him an appraising glance. "It looks good on you—a word of advice. You need to own your look. If you feel nervous, then you'll look nervous. But your confidence will shine through if you feel like you are rocking your look."

"Thanks, Mandana. And thank you for the fake girlfriend pic earlier, even if I didn't use it."

"You're welcome."

"Speaking of courage, could I get a rum and coke?"

Mandana smiled at him. "Sure, just how much courage do you need?"

"Um, maybe light on the courage. I want to keep a clear head."

"You got it. I need to see some identification, though."

"Really?"

"I don't plan on losing my job, not even for a stud like you." She winked.

Quincy handed over his driver's license, which was returned with a rum and coke. "Thank you. What do I owe you?"

"You're welcome, and I'll just charge you for the coke. Friends discount."

"Thanks." Just then, he felt a tap on his shoulder and turned around to see a vivacious young woman standing there.

"Hi, you must be Quincy. I'm Sara. Oh, can I get a Cosmo?"

Mandana nodded, "Sure, once I see some ID."

The young woman quickly handed over her license. When Sara's head was turned away, Mandana mouthed, "Twenty-three?" to Quincy, who shrugged apologetically.

Mary said her cousin was younger than me. I didn't think she was a decade younger. Well, I'm here now.

Quincy paid for their drinks and left a good tip for Mandana. Once seated, the date turned into a decidedly one-sided affair. Quincy could not remember a date where he had ever spoken less.

She is a chatterbox. I think I know everything there is to know about her. Sara is a nice girl, though. Woman, not girl. She's young, but not that young. I'm still not entirely sure why Mary set me up with her cousin, who is ten years younger than me. Do I give off that kind of vibe? Oh, no. I hope I don't. I much prefer someone around my age. Someone like Mandana, for instance.

"Want to go back to my place?"

The question brought Quincy back to reality. "I'm sorry, what?"

"Do you want to go back to my place? The drinks are much cheaper for a nightcap. The waitress probably wants to turn the table, too. I know I did when I was waiting tables."

Sara had a lot of stories from waitressing in college. I'm pretty sure she could talk all night about her experiences. Her stories are generally funny, though. This might not be my best idea ever, but this has been a fun evening so far. Let's see where it goes.

"That's very thoughtful of you."

"Thanks. I'm having so much fun with you. You're a great conversationalist."

I've spoken maybe one hundred words tonight.

"Thanks. You, too. Just a nightcap, right?"

She nodded affirmatively. Quincy paid the check, and they made their way back to Sara's apartment.

"Have a seat. Rum and coke? Beer? Cider?"

He sat down on Sara's couch. "Rum and coke, please. Light on the rum if you could."

"Good idea. We definitely don't want to make any poor choices tonight."

"Agreed. That wasn't what I meant, but it makes sense. I want to make good choices tonight. Responsible choices." Quincy looked around for something to break his stream of consciousness. "This is a nice little place—really convenient location. You have so many good restaurants nearby, plus a grocery store within walking distance. Lots of public transit, too. Have you been to a Thorns or Timbers game? Really easy to get to on transit.”

I barely said anything during dinner, and now I'm babbling. How long does it take to make a couple of drinks?

Quincy heard the click of Sara's heels in the kitchenette coming his way. “Have I asked you about—” His mouth stopped working when he saw Sara settling down next to him. She didn't have any drinks. She also had no clothes besides a garter belt, stockings, and heels.

“Sorry, I decided I was done drinking alcohol tonight. I want to put my mouth to better use.” Sara leaned in, and Quincy felt her lips caress his jawline.

“Sara, I don't want to give you the wrong idea, but—”

“Shhh, it's okay, Quincy. I like you a lot, but I'm not ready for a commitment right now, and I'm *definitely* not ready for a family. We know this isn't going further, so let's enjoy tonight.” Sara returned to nuzzling his neck, her hands plucking at his shirt.

“Are you sure you want to do this?”

“Quincy, don't overthink this. You're hot, and it's been a while since I've been with someone. I want you to help me out, and I want to help you out. If you aren't interested, then we can call it a night and go our separate ways with no *hard* feelings. Otherwise, I've got a better use for your mouth.” Sara presented Quincy with a bare breast, just an inch from his mouth.

“Fuck it, why not? How often do I have a pretty and naked woman in my lap?”

"That's the spirit," Sara moaned as he latched his mouth on the proffered nipple and proceeded to nibble and suck.

Quincy used one hand to help Sara balance while the other explored her trimmed mound. Their lips locked as he explored her curves, caressing her ass while intermittently returning to her soaked slit. He lifted himself so Sara could tug off his shirt and pants. They both sighed as she positioned him at her entrance and sank down on his hardness.

"I'm safe, so don't worry about any more kids. Just enjoy it. Mmm, I am."

Later that night, as they separated for a second time, Sara panted, "You are amazing. Thank you very much, Quincy. I'm worn out, though, and we're not doing the sleeping over thing."

"Gotcha. Thank you, Sara, for an...invigorating evening. This was a good time. I need to go pick up Ruby soon anyway."

"It was, but so you know, I'm going to tell my cousin we just had dinner but no chemistry. Okay?"

"Makes sense to me. One-time thing, no need to make it complicated."

"It doesn't need to be complicated...or one time." Sara gave him a satisfied grin. "Call me sometime if you're in a dry spell. Maybe we can help each other out again, no strings attached."

"Uh, sure. I'll keep you in mind."

"Good night, Quincy."

"Good night, Sara."

Quincy texted Tasha to say he was on his way. When he got to her place, he started to apologize, but Tasha shushed him.

"Way to go, stud."

"What do you mean?"

"Quincy, you smell like pussy and sweat."

"Oh."

"It's cool. Maybe you can return the favor and babysit for Megan and me at a later date. We have to keep the volume down when Sophia is around, you know?" Tasha leered at him. "I *really* want to make Megan scream."

"I definitely owe you one, so sure."

"Ruby has been an angel. By the way, I apologize in advance, but Sophia showed Ruby some roller derby videos, so I expect we will all be going to a roller derby game soon."

Quincy chuckled. "I think I can handle roller derby."

Chapter 4
Free Fallin'
Tom Petty

Freezing rain sucks. This whole situation sucks. I can do better than this.

Mandana was sitting in her increasingly cold apartment, reviewing the last few days in her head. Growing up on the East Coast, Mandana was familiar with snow, but freezing rain had been relatively uncommon and short-lived. She certainly was not mentally prepared for multiple days in a row of freezing rain, which shut down the city.

Thinking back to Friday, when this whole disaster started, she reminisced on the cascading chain of bad decisions. First, the restaurant had opened, which was a bad idea. Schools had let off three hours early, but the rain was minimal by early afternoon when management decided to have evening service. As the rain picked up, only a handful of patrons came for dinner, which meant the place was overstaffed. Management decided to stay open rather than shut down early to compensate for lost business hopefully. By the night's end, public transit was down, and the roads were a mess, so getting home was challenging and very expensive for many staff.

Power went down overnight, so the restaurant lost its food, and no deliveries were coming. Management sent emails and texts informing staff there was no work until further notice. There would be no compensation for lost hours. Mandana was pissed about the compensation part. Not so much for herself, as she had amassed a sizable nest egg over the past decade, but for other staff who didn't have savings. She knew some of the cooks and servers would be hard-pressed to cover rent because of this.

Mandana lost power on Monday and, by Tuesday morning, was living in an icebox. She carefully hoarded power for her phone and tablet and kept her refrigerator shut. Mandana bundled herself in blankets and read books by sunlight during the day and candlelight at night. When power was restored late on Tuesday afternoon, she started working on a business plan. Mandana had been idly thinking of opening a bar, restaurant, or even a coffee shop of her own for years, but now she was in the mood to make it happen. Her number one priority would be to treat the people who worked for her fairly and respectfully. Mandana promised herself that her staff wouldn't have to worry about covering rent in a future ice storm or blizzard.

She called her parents to tell them about her idea to start a business, but she had to leave a voicemail. Wanting someone to talk to, she called Megan.

"Hey, Mandana, what's up?"

"Hi, Megan. I needed someone to talk to. I've got an idea, but I also wanted to check and see how you all were doing."

"We are good so far. We lost power for maybe an hour on Friday night but have been lucky so far. What about you?"

"I was without power for about a day. It wasn't fun, but I didn't get frostbite or anything. Some people have been without for days. I feel lucky I only lost power for a day."

"It's still hard, though."

"Yeah. I miss doing yoga with you. Two of our classes together were canceled because of the weather."

"Tasha and I were just about to do some yoga—"

Mandana heard an explosive snort and laughter, presumably from Tasha.

"Is yoga a euphemism for sex?"

"No, um...Sophia is in her bed with the cats, and, uh..."

"You can say it. Trust me, I'm a bartender. You wouldn't believe all the stuff I've heard over the years. Nothing you say will surprise me."

Megan sighed. "Fine. We are about to do naked yoga."

"So, exercise and foreplay at the same time? I like it."

"I guess that's one way to put it—Tasha, stop it."

"Do you want her to stop whatever it is?"

"No, not really." Megan's breathing was getting ragged.

Mandana laughed. "Well, I'm going to let you go so you can do some naked yoga with your fiancée. I think I might do yoga as well, although I don't think I will have as much fun as you will."

"Uh, huh. Sure. Sounds great. Talk to you tomorrow—mmpf."

Mandana chuckled to herself as she got her yoga mat and laid it on the floor. Then, she walked into her bedroom to change into yoga clothes.

Hmm, or I could just do it naked. There's no one else here, and it might be fun. Plus, why go through the extra effort of taking clothes off, then putting different clothes on, and then getting those clothes all sweaty? See, doing it naked is better for the environment.

Ninety minutes later, Mandana slid into the shower feeling sensual and invigorated. Naked yoga felt strange at first, especially as her breasts were free to move according to the dictates of physics, but overall, it felt terrific. Toweling off after, Mandana reached for nightclothes.

Or, I could just not wear them. It just feels...different. Again, there's no one else here, so why not? Damn, I really should have closed the curtains. Hopefully, someone enjoyed the show.

Mandana closed the blinds and then curled up on the couch to watch a movie. She wasn't feeling anything serious, so she found an action movie. It was dumb but fun, and the cast was attractive.

Relaxing nude was a new experience for her, and she found herself a bit more charged than usual.

Before getting in bed, Mandana pulled a couple of items out of her toy drawer and used them to bring herself to an orgasm before falling asleep. Waking up the following day to another rainy forecast, she languidly used her toys again, taking her time rather than succumbing to the urgency she felt the previous night. She brought herself to two more orgasms before finally rolling out of bed. Mandana was finishing her coffee when the phone rang.

She picked up, "Hey, Megan."

"Hi, Mandana. Um, sorry about last night. That was probably a bit much."

"Don't worry, Megan. You and Tasha are adults, and honestly, it's kinda hot."

"I thought you said—"

"I did. I'm not into women, but you are both beautiful, and I can appreciate the eroticism. Kind of like artistic lesbian porn. It's not what gets me off, but I appreciate it anyway."

"Thanks, I think."

They both laughed. "Just to be clear, I'm not suggesting you make artistic lesbian porn."

"But you would watch it if we did?" Megan teased.

Mandana chuckled. "Naughty. I like it. And yes, I would."

"Good to know."

"So, confession time."

"Oh?"

"After you hung up last night, I decided to try nude yoga on my own."

"What did you think?"

"It was weird at first, but I kinda like it. Actually, I haven't put clothes on since."

"Wow, I didn't see that coming."

"That's what she said." Mandana snorted at her own bad joke. "Seriously, though, it's kinda, I dunno, freeing. I just feel different, more alive, I guess. Do you think I'm weird?"

"No, it sounds liberating and refreshing. Now I want to try it. I just don't feel like I should do it while Sophia is around."

"I get that."

"Quincy apparently owes us about a day of watching Sophia. We may try the whole *au naturel* thing."

"Among other things, I'm sure."

Mandana could practically hear Megan's blush over the phone. "Yes, Tasha has a lot of ideas for what we could do."

"I bet. She seems very creative. Hey, speaking of things to do, have you ever considered teaching nude yoga classes?"

Megan gasped. "No, I can't say I have, but it's an exciting idea. It seems like a very Portland thing to do."

"Yes, very Portland. It's very LA, too. If you decide to do it, then I will definitely try it at least once. It was liberating to practice nude yoga on my own, but I'm not sure if I could do it in front of other people, especially guys."

Megan mused, "What if I taught an all-female class? Or an LGBTQ+-friendly class for women and those who identify that way?"

"That's a good call. It sounds like you're thinking about it."

"I am now. I know I would have at least two students."

"Who's the other…" She paused as realization struck. "Oh, Tasha. Right."

"Didn't you have something you wanted to talk about?"

Mandana shifted into serious business mode, her voice losing its flirty edge. "I did. I'm considering opening a pub, which I know is probably a bad idea."

Megan grunted softly. "Why?"

"Because the failure rate for restaurants is enormous. Plus, Portland is a foodie city so that competition would be fierce."

"Those are quality points to consider. What makes your pub distinct?"

Mandana's shoulders dropped as she sighed, "Honestly, that's something I'm struggling with. I'm considering a Persian theme, but anything remotely Middle Eastern could be problematic given American history with Iran since the revolution, along with other issues in the area."

"Also, a good point. What about a cat cafe? I mean, not a pub, but a coffee shop."

"That's an interesting proposition. A coffee shop was one idea I considered." Mandana paused to think. "And I like cats. It would mean possibly having nights off, which is a strange concept for me."

"You would have time to go out on dates if you wanted to."

Mandana's voice dropped an octave. "Megan, you're not planning on setting me up with someone, are you?"

"Definitely not. I don't know anyone to set you up with anyway."

"That's good to hear. I've never been a fan of blind dates."

"I went on a couple of blind double dates with Tasha back in college. I made her go out on a couple of blind double dates with me as well. It wasn't great. Actually, that's how I met my now ex-husband. He was the wingman for the guy Tasha was going out with."

"Speaking of Tasha and blind dates, any idea how the blind date went for Quincy and what's her face?"

"So-so, I think. He said the age gap was too much for dating, but she took him back to hers for a *nightcap*."

"I assume you mean sex." Mandana pursed her lips. "Hmm. Interesting. I'm pretty good at reading people, and I didn't see him as a one-night-stand kind of guy."

"Tasha said he looked embarrassed when he came to pick up Ruby afterward. Maybe he didn't see himself as a one-night-stand kind of guy, either."

"Possibly. His date was pretty hot, and people do stupid things for sex all of the time." Mandana shook her head. "Enough about Quincy. I should consider this cat cafe idea. If you have any other bright ideas, please tell me."

"Will do. I'm going to look into your nude yoga class idea…" There was a pause before Megan came back. "Of course, Tasha walks in right then. Now I've gotten my fiancée all hot and bothered again."

"You might need to take care of her."

"Nope, Sophia is up. We have rules."

"Poor Tasha."

"Hey, what about me?" Megan exclaimed.

Chapter 5
Evil Woman
Black Sabbath

Quincy picked up Ruby after school on the Friday of the storm. The three-hour early release made for a strange day, but that was better than having her trapped at school for hours because of bad weather. After he finished work, they hunkered down with books and board games to ride out the freezing rain. The ice storm knocked out power for Quincy and Ruby on Sunday morning, but not for too long. Electricity was restored by Sunday afternoon, and Quincy was confident about being able to work on Monday morning. Late Sunday evening, a message went out about schools closing the next day, so he was prepared to take care of her while working. Those preparations paid off as school ended up being canceled all week. By the end of the week, Quincy was incredibly thankful Ruby was such a bookworm, able to sit quietly for most of the time he worked. It helped that Dolly Purrton spent most of her time with Ruby.

What Quincy was totally unprepared for was an email on Saturday morning from Stacy, his ex-girlfriend and Ruby's mother, whom he hadn't heard from in years. Stacy was coming to Portland soon and was prepared to demand full custody of Ruby to take her to live permanently with Stacy and her new husband in Jacksonville. This unpleasant missive sent Quincy into a panic. He frantically searched the internet for guidance and potential legal counsel. Quincy was strongly considering ditching his Saturday afternoon fundraiser planning meeting with Mary and Tasha but decided it would be a functional distraction from the terror he felt.

Once again, he took Ruby over to Tasha's place, where Megan would look after her during his meeting. Tasha met him downstairs, and they walked up to her apartment where she let them in. Ruby immediately abandoned Quincy to go and sit with Sophia, which he thought was adorable.

I'm so glad she has found a new friend. I'm also happy I get along so well with Megan and Tasha. Being friends with the parents of Ruby's friends is easier, for sure.

Quincy looked up from observing his daughter to see Mandana and Megan in the kitchenette. Mandana gave him a finger wave and said, "Hey, stud. Good to see you again."

He felt blood rush to his cheeks. "Hi, Mandy. Good to see you as well."

Megan had a quizzical look as she asked, "Mandy?"

"It's easier for people to say than Mandana. Especially when they are drunk. Quincy learned about my work name when he and his date got drinks from me."

"Oh, so that's why you said his date was twenty-three."

"Seriously, you all have been talking about my blind date?"

Megan harrumphed, "In our defense, there wasn't much to talk about during the ice storm. So, yes, your blind date with a twenty-three-year-old came up."

"Hey, in *my defense*, I didn't know she was ten years younger than me. Mary forgot to mention that tidbit." In his already fragile state, Quincy could feel his blood pressure surging.

Tasha jumped in, sensing the potential for rising tension. "Are you seeing her again?"

"No, she isn't interested in anything permanent and doesn't want to do the whole family thing at her age, which I completely understand since I wasn't planning on raising a kid when I was her age, either." *I can hear the snippiness of my voice. I need to get my shit together before I lose the only friends I seem to have at the moment.*

"But you still..."

Quincy was pretty sure half of the blood in his body was now in his cheeks, which were probably glowing with embarrassment by now. "She initiated, and it was recreational between two consenting adults. No strings, no follow-up, just a good time. Well, good times."

"Well, good for you for handling that maturely. Now, can you possibly watch Sophia all day tomorrow? Because Megan and I have some things to catch up on." Tasha's voice dropped a few registers. "*A lot of things.*"

"I would be happy to watch her. I certainly owe you."

"Great. Can we drop her off around seven-thirty? Megan is thinking of teaching nude yoga, so the three of us want to go to an early morning nude yoga class to try out a class."

An awkward silence followed, with each adult looking nervously at the others.

Mandana recovered first, saying, "Good job, Tasha. I think you broke the poor man's brain."

Feverishly wishing a hole would suddenly appear in the floor to swallow him, Quincy barely managed to utter, "Seven-thirty is fine. We should probably go now. Right now. For our meeting with Mary. Which happens very soon."

Quincy stumbled out the door, assuming Tasha would follow along soon. She joined him a couple of minutes later, and they walked silently over to the coffee house to meet Mary. Embarrassment and the terror of losing Ruby turned Quincy's brain into a mess. He knew he was spiraling, but he couldn't stop.

As they walked toward the cafe, Tasha suddenly halted and rounded on Quincy. "What the hell, dude? Where is your head at? There's no way I can keep up with Mary's firehose of ideas on my own. I need your support."

"I'm really sorry, Tasha. My mind is on something else. Something that has to be my primary focus right now. I'm sorry."

Tasha's mood altered instantly, and she sounded concerned when she asked, "Do you want to talk about it?"

"I don't know. It's a serious thing, and I don't want to burden you with it."

"Hey, I can be a good listener. Sometimes, talking something out helps."

His shoulders slumped as he shuffled along. "Okay, here goes. Ruby's mom emailed me today. She wants full custody of Ruby and wants to move her to Jacksonville."

"Are you shitting me? Has your ex helped raise Ruby at all?"

"No, she basically ran the moment she left the hospital. Ruby has never met her, and I've never wanted her to. Stacy went down some bad roads after she left us."

"You've kept in touch?"

"No. I get the occasional update from Stacy's parents, but that's it. This just blindsided me this morning. I've been a wreck ever since."

"Wow. I'm so sorry I bit your head off earlier. You have a heavy load to carry. Do you have a lawyer to help fight this?"

"No, not yet. I tried looking online, but it's all so much...I'm feeling overwhelmed right now. I can't even think about it, which I know is bad, which makes me anxious, and now I feel like I'm in this doom loop."

"I'll call Mary and tell her something came up and reschedule. Come back to the apartment and stay with us for a bit. I need to make another phone call. Talk with Megan. She's been through some shit recently and might be able to help."

"Thanks, Tasha."

They entered the apartment to find Mandana and Megan sitting on the couch, watching a Disney movie with the two girls on the floor, each with a snuggling cat.

Megan looked surprised. "You two are back early. Is everything okay?"

Tasha beckoned them over before quietly answering, "Quincy can tell you more, but he's not in a good place right now. I need to call Maria."

"Oh, shit. You sound concerned. It must be bad if you're calling Maria."

I'm not sure who this Maria person is, but she definitely seems to know the right people. I certainly hope she knows a lawyer who's as good with custody battles as the boutique owner was with outfits.

"Yeah, it's bad." Tasha inquired, "Quincy, do you want some tea or something?"

Megan was already in motion as she rattled off the options. "We have water, tea, coffee, hot chocolate, or hard cider. What sounds good?"

Mandana trailed in her wake, pulling a chair back at the table and guiding Quincy into it.

"Tea sounds good, but hard cider might be perfect, thank you."

"Coming right up."

"Megan, why don't you go and sit with Quincy while I fix us drinks? Making drinks and listening is something I'm quite skilled at, after all." Mandana's professional air allowed for no disagreement.

"Will do. Let me quickly check on the girls to make sure they're okay. I suspect we don't want them interrupting us." Megan was gone, then swiftly returned, sitting down across the table from Quincy. "All right, what's up?"

He took a deep breath and started, "Stacy, Ruby's mother, emailed me this morning. She's coming here to get custody of Ruby. Apparently, Stacy has a husband now, and they live in Jacksonville."

"Florida?" Megan asked rhetorically. "That's a long haul. I can understand why you are upset. Can you tell us about your relationship with Stacy?"

"After college, I got a job in Houston. I was young and stupid, and the job paid well. *Incredibly well.* It had to be because the hours were long, and the stress was catastrophic. Anyway, like I said, I was young, stupid, and wasn't making good decisions—lots of alcohol and drugs. Mostly speed to keep me awake and going. With some cocaine on the side. That's when I met Stacy."

Quincy paused as Mandana handed him a Two Towns cider, then passed one to Megan before seating herself.

"We liked the same clubs, the same booze, the same drugs. Plus, I had a nice apartment, and she liked money. We dated for about a year before she got pregnant. I'm not even sure how we managed to go a year because she was usually too high to remember the pill, and we were both usually too high to remember condoms. Anyway, once her parents found out she was pregnant, her mom threw her into rehab. I got clean as well and started to get my life together."

Quincy took a long drink from his bottle before continuing. "It turns out that once you took away the clubs, the alcohol, and the drugs, Stacy and I had nothing in common."

Mandana put a gentle hand on his arm. "I can tell you I've seen a lot of similar situations, being a bartender. It's sad and usually not pretty when everything ends. It's worse when it's your co-workers because it always seems to drag everyone in. Sorry I interrupted your story."

"No problem. The only thing we had in common was this kid in her belly. Unfortunately, Stacy wanted no part of her, either. After Ruby was born, Stacy left. She ran off to Miami and got back into the drugs and booze. I keep in touch with her parents out of courtesy, but they really don't like me. I think they blame me for the corruption of their little angel, even though Stacy was already a mess by the time we met. So, I've sort of kept tabs on Stacy through them. I haven't heard from Stacy herself since she asked me for money about five years ago. Ruby has never met her, and I am not sure I want her to."

Megan looked a bit hurt by that but nodded. "I understand why you kept Ruby's mother away. When I left Brad, my ex-husband, I was furious with him. I didn't necessarily want to keep Sophia from seeing him, but I wouldn't have been upset about it, either."

"It sounds like you've changed your mind about him."

"I have. Our leaving, plus the divorce, was a wake-up call for Brad. Tasha also gave him a piece of her mind, which seemed to help him reorient himself. He appears to be getting his life together. I'm still not done being angry with him, but his stupidity brought me back to Tasha." Megan smiled contentedly. "That's obviously working out wonderfully, so there's been positives for me."

"I did get one big positive, Ruby. I'm not even angry with Stacy, or at least I wasn't until this morning. We were both young and stupid. Now, I am terrified I might lose Ruby."

Megan nodded in understanding. "I'm sorry, Quincy. Tasha is probably on the phone with Maria, and she can be a big help."

"Who is Maria?"

"She's a friend of Tasha's. An ex-girlfriend, actually. She's also a *badass* divorce lawyer. When I say badass, I mean Maria is the divorce lawyer other divorce lawyers have nightmares about. She helped me with my divorce, although I'm pretty sure she thinks I was much too nice to Brad. Anyway, Maria has a ton of connections. If anyone can help you, it's her."

"I really hope so. I haven't told Ruby yet. She has always been curious about her mother. I haven't lied, but I never told her the full truth, either. I planned to eventually when she is older and hopefully better able to understand how her parents were drugged out of their minds. Circumstances might mean I need to tell her sooner, and I worry about how she'll take it. I love her with all of my heart. I don't want her to think she was unwanted or a mistake."

Megan reached over and grabbed his hand, saying, "I totally understand. I tried...Brad and I both tried very hard to make sure Sophia knew we both loved her and our split had nothing to do with her."

Mandana laid her hand on top of theirs, adding, "I understand your apprehension, and I think your concern makes you a good father. My parents were never emotionally warm, and I think some-times, growing up, I questioned whether they loved me. I know they did, although they are definitely not pleased with many of my life choices, but they do still love me. They just aren't very good at expressing it. You seem to have no problems in that regard."

Quincy placed his other hand on top of Mandana's. "Why do you think they had trouble expressing their love?"

"Partially because of just who they are. Very driven, work-focused people. Part of it might be their upbringing and history. We're part of a religious minority, and they were both still kids when their families fled Iran during the revolution. Even now, we don't have a place in the Persian diaspora because of our religion."

"Do you mind if I ask what religion?"

"It's fine. We're Zoroastrians. Well, I'm pretty much an atheist, which is one of those life choices my parents disapprove of. Zoroas-trianism is an ancient monotheistic faith centered in Persia. After the Muslim conquest, the religion went into decline, and there aren't many of us left, which, again, upsets my parents because I'm not practicing. Nor do I have any interest in marrying a nice Zoroastrian man, despite their best efforts."

"I can honestly say I have never heard of Zoroastrianism before today."

Megan chimed in, "Me either."

"I'm glad I can be informative," Mandana responded with a smile.

Tasha walked back into the room and joined them at the table. Mandana slid a bottle of cider over as Tasha sat down. They looked at her expectantly.

"Thanks." Tasha nodded at Mandana and took a drink. "I spoke with Maria. She wants to meet you, Quincy. I don't think she'll take your case. Her clientele is primarily women. All women, as far as I know. She did have some initial thoughts, though. You probably have an advantage because you have been Ruby's sole caretaker. Your ex has an advantage because she is the mother. Legally, motherhood isn't beneficial; however, judgments tend to favor the mother. In large part, it will be a judgment about who can better provide a safe and stable home for Ruby."

"Oh. Stability makes sense, obviously. I feel like I provide a safe and secure home already since I've taken care of Ruby from day one while Stacy has spent most of the last eight years high."

Megan countered, "Yeah, but you both have a lot of bad decisions in your past, which you just told us about. If she has gotten clean, then past substance abuse could be a wash."

Quincy hated how quickly Megan identified the problem, but he knew she was right. He and Stacy both had histories of substance abuse. He may have cleaned up first, but if they were both clean, it was a matter of timing. Then, he had another thought. "Stacy has a husband now. Do you think being married will matter?"

Tasha responded, "Maria didn't mention marriage, but it makes sense. If there is an implicit bias toward the mother in judgments, then it stands to reason there is probably something similar in favor of a married parent."

"*Shit*. Rachel was my longest relationship since Ruby was born, and that's over. I'm not sure when this will happen, but there's no way I can get married in a short time."

Mandana asked, "What if you were engaged?"

"As a young single dad, I'm supposedly attractive to women." Quincy shrugged. "Attractive at first, but none seemed interested in sticking around for long. I've been told I am too devoted to my daughter. If I can't keep a girlfriend, I'm not sure how I'll manage to have a fiancée."

"I meant a fake fiancée."

Quincy stared at Mandana in disbelief. "Hire an actress to pretend to be my fiancée?"

She shrugged, throwing her hands in the air. "Something like that."

He snorted, "I wish I had enough money to hire someone."

"What about Sara?"

Quincy arched his eyebrows at Mandana. "Even if she hadn't made it clear she wasn't interested, I'm not sure being engaged—well, fake engaged—to someone ten years younger than me makes a strong case for stability."

"He makes a good point, Mandana," Megan interjected. "Quincy needs to be fake engaged to someone smart, successful, and mature."

Quincy nodded in agreement.

Tasha followed up with, "Someone like you, Mandana."

There was silence after Tasha's bombshell, broken only by the sounds of the movie the girls were watching.

Mandana recovered first. "I'm a bartender. I don't think that counts for stability."

Megan countered, "You are a bartender who wants to open a small business. By the way, the cat cafe idea sounds better the more I think about it."

Mandana mused, "I think it's a phenomenal idea, too. Plus, there's not much direct competition in the Portland market. Similar businesses have succeeded in other cities."

Quincy couldn't help himself. "You could call it The Purrfect Cup. Oh, I know—The Purrsian Paradise. See what I did there with Persian and purring?" Quincy knew he was grinning like an idiot but couldn't contain his enthusiasm for making puns.

Mandana tried to hold back a laugh, which turned into a snort, which then made everyone else laugh, which made Mandana laugh. "Thank you for confirming that dad jokes are a thing. Those are good names, though. I genuinely like the second one."

"Thanks."

"Did you come up with it right now?"

"I did."

"Clever and funny. Good-looking, too."

Quincy felt an electric shiver traverse his nervous system. *She thinks I'm good-looking? And she likes my dad jokes?*

Mandana tapped her lips thoughtfully. "The fake fiancée thing might not be a terrible idea. Let me think about it."

"Really?" Megan, Quincy, and Tasha asked simultaneously and with varying degrees of disbelief.

"I'm not saying 'Yes.' I'm thinking about it."

"It's totally up to you, but I would be forever grateful if you did," Quincy said, trying to play it cool. Internally, his emotions were roiling.

Mandana settled into the role of a powerful businesswoman who held all the cards. "Let's say I agree to do this. It is strictly platonic. There will be no feelings and definitely no sex. Oh, and you pay for our dates."

"Dates?"

"It has to look legitimate, right? It would look strange if we got engaged without ever going out on a date, don't you think?"

"Fake dating makes sense. I accept those terms."

"We'll watch Ruby," Megan added enthusiastically.

Quincy added, "I could also help with the website for The Purrsian Paradise. I'm not great with the front-end stuff, but I'm really good with the underlying code. I can create an app for it, too."

Tasha interjected, "How did I not know you do coding? I excel at the client-facing side but struggle with those back-end functions."

He laughed. "At first, I was too busy unsuccessfully hitting on you, and then we were too busy planning for a fundraiser."

"You were hitting on my fiancée?" Megan asked but didn't seem too upset about it. Quincy thought she looked a bit proud.

"I mean, Tasha is gorgeous, so you can't blame me for trying. Um, you are both gorgeous as well."

"Oh, so I'm gorgeous, but not gorgeous enough to hit on?" Quincy could see Mandana's eyes narrowing dangerously.

"Um, I'm not saying I wouldn't flirt with you, I feel like it would be awkward, you know—"

"I'm just giving you a hard time, Que."

"Que?" Quincy scrunched his eyes and bared his teeth in an involuntary wince.

Mandana shook her head ruefully. "Yeah, once I said it, I didn't like it. I'll think about a good nickname for you."

"Um, don't feel like you have to, Mandana."

She smiled at him impishly before turning to Megan and Tasha. "All right, friends. I'm going to head out. I need to take a nap before work. Ladies, I will see you tomorrow for yoga."

After Mandana left, the remaining adults joined the kids and watched the remainder of the movie. Once the credits rolled, Tasha went to help Ruby put on her coat while Megan pulled Quincy aside.

"Are you feeling better?"

"A little. I feel like this whole situation is so unfair. Stacy left us. While I was changing diapers, Stacy was getting wasted. I was there for Ruby's first steps, her first words, her first day of school. Every single milestone in Ruby's life, *I have been there*, and now Stacy wants to swoop in and take her away from me. *Fuck* that shit."

"It sucks, and it isn't remotely fair. Tasha and I are here for you. Quincy, as much as this hurts, I'm glad you are fighting for your little girl. You seem like a great father, and that's important. Trust me, I know."

"Thanks, Megan. I appreciate it. Do you want me to pick up Sophia tomorrow, or will you all bring her over?"

"That's sweet of you to offer. We will bring her over in the morning. Is seven-thirty okay?"

"Seven-thirty is fine. I'll make breakfast for the girls. Are there any allergies I should know about? Does Sophia like pancakes?"

"Sophia *loves* pancakes. That's probably her favorite breakfast. She is allergic to bee stings, but bees shouldn't be a problem this time of year."

"Perfect. I can watch her as long as you want. Tasha hinted she is interested in some alone time with you."

Megan turned a brilliant shade of scarlet. "Thanks, um…we will keep your offer in mind. Now I'm going to strangle my fiancée."

Quincy chuckled as he went to collect Ruby. They said their goodbyes and headed home. Not long after they got home, his phone buzzed with a text. It was Tasha's friend, Maria, who was asking to meet him for lunch on Tuesday. He responded, agreeing to meet her. She told him where and when she wanted to meet him, and he complied.

Chapter 6

Take A Chance On Me

ABBA

Mandana stripped off her clothes as soon as she returned home after yoga. Nude yoga was very enjoyable, and the trio went out for a quick coffee afterward. Mandana didn't want to tarry as she sensed Megan and Tasha were feeling sexually charged after their class. Osmosing their energy got Mandana fired up as well. She pulled out a clit vibrator and her favorite curved steel dildo before laying back on her bed, slowly pleasuring herself.

Mmm, nude yoga was excellent. It was fun seeing Megan and Tasha doing it as well. I'm definitely not into them, but I can certainly admire both their beauty and their form. Oh, that feels good. This whole naturist thing is working for me. I feel more confident, relaxed, and horny. Very horny. It's been a while since I have had the real thing. Why did Quincy pop into my head when I thought about getting some cock? He is cute. There we go, Que Tee. That's his nickname. Oh, damn, that feels good. Right there. Oh...Yes...

An unknown number of orgasms later, Mandana was ready for a nap and then lunch. As she ate, she thought about Quincy and the fake fiancée idea.

Why am I even considering this? I've met this guy twice. Sure, he seems nice enough, and he clearly cares a lot about his daughter. Is he really so nice, though? He goes out on a blind date with a woman barely out of college and has a one-night stand. Who does that? Oh, right, someone who hasn't gotten laid in a while. A single father raising a young girl, he may not get many shots, and Sara was good-looking. Is that a good example to set, though? Okay, focus. What's in this for me? Not much. I might get some free help for a website for a business I haven't set up. Yet. Screw it, I'm tired of working for someone else. The cat cafe sounds like a lot of fun, and I could have my nights free—such a strange concept after all these years. And, yes, I could go out on actual dates with people who work regular hours, like Quincy. I'm back to him again. In conclusion, there is no good reason for me to be his fake fiancée. On the other hand, there's no good reason for me not to do it besides the blatantly obvious reason that it's weird. Right. Fuck it. I came to Portland for something different, and this is as different as it gets.

> Mandana: *Once you are done making Tasha breathe through her ears, text me Quincy's number. Also, can you watch Ruby tomorrow night?*

Right as Mandana was about to leave for work, she got an answering text.

> Megan: *LOL. Tasha needs gills. Sure. Here's his number.*

Mandana grinned, chuckling to herself. "Wow. Thank you, Megan, for taking time out from sex." Once she got Quincy's number, she texted him.

> Mandana: *Date tomorrow night. Megan will watch Ruby. Thai or Indian?*

> Quincy: *I like both. Thai works.*

> *Is this a real date or a fake date?*

> Mandana: *It's an interview.*

> Quincy: *Got it.*

Mandana sent him the time and place to meet the following evening. The next day, she contacted a commercial realtor and set up a meeting for a loan at the bank. Mandana drove herself around various locations to see what kind of neighborhood vibe spoke to her. She also contacted local cat shelters to inquire about a potential partnership. It was a busy and tiring day, and she wasn't entirely sure she still wanted to see Quincy tonight.

I asked him, so I really should follow through. I also need to figure out something to wear. What is the right tone to set? Business, for sure. Not too much business, though. Business hot. That's a thing, right? I have the perfect outfit.

Mandana arrived ten minutes early, dressed to kill in black and red, with silver jewelry accenting her outfit. She was pleasantly surprised to see Quincy already there. He was wearing a sport coat, slacks, and dress shirt and smiled when he saw her.

Good job, Quincy. He made an effort and is taking this seriously. We are way overdressed for this place, but we're fine. I'm still on the fence about this idea, but slightly closer to 'Yes.'

"Hi, Mandana. You look lovely tonight."

"Hi, and you clean up nicely yourself. Are you ready?"

"Definitely."

Quincy pulled her chair out for her as they were seated before taking his own seat.

A bit too much effort. It feels like he's trying too hard. I appreciate the effort, but I question the sincerity.

Mandana perused the menu before asking, "What looks good to you?"

"Lots of things. How do you feel about an appetizer?"

"An appetizer sounds good. What were you thinking of?"

"Satay, if that works for you, of course."

"I like satay."

"Great. I hope it is satay-sfactory."

Mandana groaned at the pun.

"Sorry, I should have resisted the urge."

"No, it's fine. Honestly, it was pretty funny, but I felt like laughing would simply reward you, and I'm not sure rewards would be wise. You might stick me with more puns."

Quincy laughed. "Stick, satay. Nice one. Thank you for not running away screaming."

"Yet," Mandana grunted.

"Got it. I'll try to contain myself."

"Please don't. I'm not saying I agree with this ludicrous plan; however, I would like to get to know the real you, puns and all. Just in case I lose my mind and say, 'Yes.' At least I'll know what I'm getting myself into."

"Thank you. I appreciate your honesty, Mandana. Realistically, I don't expect you will agree to this. It's very sweet you are even considering it, especially since this is, what, the third time we've met?"

"Exactly what I said to myself. So, what are you ordering?"

"I think I want the Pad See Ew, with medium spiciness."

"An interesting choice. Pad Kee Mao for me."

Quincy looked back at the menu. "I was thinking about Kee Mao, but I'm in a broccoli mood tonight."

"Weirdo. No one is ever in a broccoli mood. Why medium spiciness?"

He pouted. "Well, I can handle the hot level, but sometimes I feel like the spice overwhelms the flavor. I usually go mild or medium. I get the spice but can still taste the main dish."

She bobbed her head thoughtfully. "Makes sense. So, why medium over mild?"

"Honestly, I didn't want you to think I can't handle spicy foods."

That actually sounds like the honest answer. He could have gone hot or even Thai hot to show off. Instead he went for a practical balance. Once again, good work, Quincy.

After they ordered, Mandana decided it was time to start grilling Quincy. "Let's talk about Sara."

"What would you like to know?" Quincy's tone was light, but his expression looked guarded.

"Why did you go back to her place?"

"*Wow.* Not starting with the easy questions, are you? It's fair, though." Quincy didn't look happy. "We were having a nice evening. It's been a long time since I went on a date with a woman who wasn't a parent. Sara was a talker, so I didn't say much, but she was pleasant and engaging. I guess when she asked me to come over, I didn't want the night to end."

"How did you end up in bed?"

"When we got there, she offered to make us drinks. I sat down on the couch. Next thing I knew, she was sitting beside me wearing stockings and nothing else."

"And then you just fucked?"

Quincy made an exasperated face. "What did you expect me to do? If it makes you feel better, I asked Sara if she was sure before anything happened. She wanted me to help her scratch an itch, as consenting adults." His voice rose slightly, taking on a brittle edge as if he fought to keep from shouting. "Look, I don't usually have pretty and naked women climbing into my lap and offering me no-strings-attached sex. Actually, this was the first time it's happened since Ruby was born. Happy now?" He certainly didn't sound happy.

"And how do you feel about it now?"

"Conflicted. It was good, but I feel like a dirty old man, especially since she's ten years younger than me. I feel like maybe I took advantage of her, yet at the same time, she was the one who got naked and came on to me. I'm not used to a woman being so aggressive and demanding."

"Is being sexually assertive a bad thing?"

"No, I'm not saying that."

"So, you are fine with a young woman barely out of college just climbing naked onto an older man and screwing him?"

Quincy looked uncomfortable as Mandana pressed the attack. "I mean, I guess so."

"What if you found out that Ruby did the same thing fifteen years from now?"

He got angry. "Wait, what? No, that's not okay."

"So, it's fine for Sara to be sexually assertive with you, but not fine for someone you care about to be assertive?"

Quincy clearly swallowed his retort, instead opting to ask, "Um, can I get a minute before I answer?"

"Take your time, Quincy."

Mandana watched Quincy as his mind worked toward an answer. Most people hated to be put on the spot like this. In Mandana's experience, men often did not react well to aggressive questioning from a woman. The question about Ruby was way out of line, and Mandana knew it. Unfortunately, she felt it was necessary to find out what sort of person Quincy was.

The satay came before Quincy finished collecting his thoughts. They finished off the appetizer in silence, including splitting the fifth and final satay in unspoken agreement.

"When Ruby grows up, I want her to feel confident and secure about herself—about her sexuality. Her happiness is the most important thing to me. If she wants to have consensual and informed recreational sex with another adult, then I want her to feel empowered to make her own choices. She is also my daughter and my whole world. I want with all of my heart to wrap her in bubble wrap and protect her from every possible danger. It is the most difficult thing I can imagine to balance my desire for her to be safe with the knowledge that she needs to make her own decisions. Do those competing interests make sense?"

"It does. I don't have your frame of reference, but I get it. Well, I get it as much as I can. After putting your thoughts into words, how do you feel about yourself?"

"I feel like I've been wrung out."

"I meant about your evening with Sara."

"Oh. Better, I guess. It's not something I want to make a habit of. It was fun, and honestly, really good sex, but I feel like it would be better with someone I care deeply about."

He responded with a generally good series of answers, but more importantly, he reined himself in, kept his cool, and didn't freak out.

"I'm sorry about pressing you so hard."

"It's okay."

"No, it's not. My question about Ruby crossed a line, and I feel bad about it. I just—"

"You needed to stress test me. I understand. You have very little reason to trust me, especially after the whole Sara thing."

"True. But, I wish I found a better way to go about it."

"Hopefully, my answer was good enough. How about we move on?"

"Sounds good."

"I know this not-a-date is you interviewing me, but am I allowed to ask questions?"

"You just did," Mandana grinned at him. "But yes, you're allowed."

"Great. Why are you even considering this whole fake fiancée thing?"

"I'm not entirely sure. Outside of some potential website help, there's no real benefit for me. We don't really know each other. The one thing I am discovering is that you are a devoted father who pulled his shit together for his daughter. Now, the woman who abandoned both of you wants to take Ruby away. Frankly, just thinking about you losing Ruby pisses me off."

Quincy laughed darkly. "It pisses me off, too."

"I know it does. It also makes you desperate enough to consider a fake engagement to a total stranger. I answered you, so it's my turn for a question. What is your favorite thing to do with Ruby?"

This time, Quincy's laugh was much lighter. "This is another hard question. I've always enjoyed going for walks or pushing her on a swing—well, I used to push her on the swing. Now she tells me she's a big girl and can do it herself." His heart melted a bit when Mandana giggled. "Movie night is always fun. Oh, and Taco Tuesdays when I don't have PTA. I think my favorite thing is reading with her. When she was a few years old, I barely had enough money to keep a roof over our heads, but I read to her every night. We started with the usual kid's books like *The Hungry Caterpillar*. Eventually, though, I would read all of my favorite books, plus books she liked. As she got older, we would take turns reading. We read the whole *American Girl* series. We read *The Hobbit*. Books were the only vacation we could afford."

"Holy shit, Quincy. Reading with your girl is a great answer. I'm guessing the *American Girl* series was your favorite."

He chuckled wryly. "Definitely. Okay, my turn. Have you ever thought about getting married or having a family?"

"I might need a minute on this, which is lucky since the food is here." Once the plates were situated, Mandana asked, "Can I try some of yours?"

"Sure, so long as you don't mind if I try some of yours."

"Deal."

They ate quietly for a bit while Mandana thought of her answer. "Yes, I've thought about getting married and having a family and decided against it. My life has never been conducive to stability, and I've made my peace with sacrificing long-term relationships. Mom and Dad have been pushing me for years to find a nice Zoroastrian man to marry, and their pressure is honestly a huge turn-off for me. Their relationship has never been great, and I don't want to follow in their footsteps. As for kids...nope. I have no interest in going through pregnancy and childbirth. Changing diapers is definitely not in the cards."

"I can tell you from experience that diaper changing is truly awful. It was like a poop volcano. Sometimes, I'd finish changing her, and I would have to do it again because she filled the diaper immediately. Oh...then there were the times when she would poop before I could get the new one on. And you can't un-smell the horrors a baby emits. Oh, and then there's the sleepless nights."

"You are making my case for me."

"True, but I still wouldn't change it. Ruby is a gift, although I think I'm fine with just her and no more."

"What about you? Do you want to get married?"

"I would like to, provided I found the right person. It's hard because I need to find someone who is both right for me and right for Ruby. Rachel checked the right boxes, but she and her husband are trying to make it work out." Quincy gave her a look which forestalled any questions. "And before you say anything, they were getting divorced when we started dating."

"She checked the right boxes, but did you love her?"

"Maybe. I don't really know. Love seems so abstract sometimes."

"I hear you. I've found companionship and enjoyment a few times, but I don't think I've ever thought it was love since I was a teenager."

"Same here."

"Okay, my turn to ask a question." Mandana paused, wanting to make it good.

"The suspense is killing me."

"Hush. What negative qualities do you bring into a relationship?"

"Ouch." Quincy clearly hadn't expected her question. "The first part of my answer is easy. My highest priority is Ruby, so any potential partner is always in second place. What else...I can be too passive. I mean, I don't advocate for myself well, and I tend to accept things like with Rachel. I really liked her, and I could have made an effort to change her mind and fight for us, but instead, I just let her go. I also need to work out more. I feel like I'm going soft in the middle. Oh, there's also my past with substance abuse, which I know is a red flag for some people. And then, no, it's stupid—"

"You can't start to say something and not finish the sentence. Don't tease me like that."

"Fine, you asked. I'm terrible at—" Quincy's voice lowered to a whisper "—eating pussy."

Mandana snorted and struggled to finish off the bite of food she was chewing without choking on it. Once she safely swallowed her food, she fanned herself with one hand while taking a drink of water with the other. "Wow, okay. I did ask. So, you're saying you struggle to eat the pink taco? You aren't a cunning linguist?" Mandana started to giggle but brought herself under control when she paid attention to Quincy's face. He looked angry and embarrassed. "I'm sorry. I shouldn't have laughed at you."

"It's fine."

"No, it's not, although I guess this goes back to the whole too-passive thing. I want you to say what you really want to say. Advocate for yourself."

Quincy tensed up. "It hurt when you laughed at me. I don't like admitting weakness; being mocked for it destroys trust and honesty. What I want from a potential partner, even a fake fiancée, is compassion and support. I don't want to be bad at eating pussy, but I feel like my lack of confidence creates this negative loop."

"That's fair, and I am sorry I laughed at you and mocked you. If you want to be a better muff diver, then it is important to have a partner who is willing to provide open and honest feedback so you know what works and what doesn't. It's not going to be me because this fake fiancée thing will be strictly platonic, but I will try to be more supportive in general."

"Apology accepted. And thank you for pushing me to advocate for myself. I actually felt terrific."

"I thought it would."

"Before I ask you a question, does this mean you are willing to be my fake fiancée?"

"Technically, you just asked a question."

"Mandana..."

Am I going to do this? This is absolutely ridiculous. And yet, Quincy seems like a genuinely good person, and he deserves the best chance possible at keeping custody of his daughter. His daughter—

"Let's say I agree to do this. What do you tell Ruby? What's my relationship with her?"

Quincy got very serious, and his body tensed as he answered. "Like I said, my number one priority is Ruby. I will tell her we are dating. We will leave the engagement part out until we are with Stacy's lawyers. I don't want to get Ruby's hopes up. I feel like she has always wanted a mother figure in her life, and I can never fill a mom-shaped hole. I don't want you filling it, either."

Ouch, that kinda hurts.

"As much as our relationship is strictly business, with no sex and no feelings, I want to make sure Ruby doesn't get attached to you, either. Then, when this is all done, and we part ways, I don't want her getting hurt. So you are to be polite and friendly to Ruby in your interactions, but nothing more. No nicknames, no affection, nothing to create attachment."

"Wow, thank you for being brutally honest." Mandana reached her hands across the table, palms up in an invitation to Quincy. He tentatively put his hands in hers. She squeezed gently. "You are a good father, and she seems like a great kid in the little bit that I've seen her. I respect what you are saying and your desire to keep her heart safe. I agree to your terms."

"Are we seriously doing this?"

"I can't believe I'm saying this, but yes. I will fake date you, and when the time comes, I will be your fake fiancée. I promise not to break Ruby's heart."

Relief flooded Quincy's voice. "*Thank you.* Thank you so much."

"You're welcome. So, what was your next question?"

"I don't even remember."

Is he crying? Yep, he's crying.

"Quincy, are you okay?"

"Yeah, sorry." He wiped his sleeve over his eyes. "This is the kindest thing anyone has ever done for me. Well, at least since Mom came and stayed with me for a couple of months after Ruby was born to teach me how to care for her."

"That's sweet. I never asked about your parents."

"Mom died during the pandemic—cancer, then COVID. Everything seemed fine, but then suddenly, she was gone. Dad hasn't been the same since. He's...distant now. He misses her a lot. We saw him over the holidays, and being around Ruby made him better, I think. I'm trying to convince him to move to Portland."

"I'm so sorry, Quincy."

"Thanks, Mandana. Um, thank you again for agreeing to be my fake fiancée. I have to go now. I'm feeling a bit overwhelmed, and I think I have to go if you don't mind. I need to hug my girl."

Mandana watched him walk over to the hostess and pay for their meal. Her eyes never left him as he opened the door to leave. She felt alone as she sat at the table, waiting for to-go boxes for their leftovers. Her loneliness mixed with a strange melancholy Mandana couldn't understand. It almost felt like she missed him.

Chapter 7
Lawyers, Guns, and Money
Warren Zevon

Quincy hurried over to Megan and Tasha's place to collect Ruby. Tasha came down to open the door. She asked, "How did it go?"

He felt his muscles stiffen and his spine locked. Quincy took a beat to relax his body, but he couldn't fully purge the tension from his voice. "Hi, Tasha. It went well. I'm sorry. I'm not in the mood to chat. I need to get Ruby and go."

"Oh, okay."

He reached out to give her hand a quick squeeze. "I'm really sorry. You're being very kind, and I'm being very rude. I promise I will explain later and make it up to you."

"Thanks, Quincy. I appreciate your honesty. We all have those days." Tasha seemed genuinely caring, and Quincy deeply appreciated their burgeoning friendship.

"Was Ruby alright?"

Tasha smiled. "She's a wonderful kid, and it's our pleasure to watch her."

"Thank you, Tasha."

Quincy enveloped Ruby in a big hug as soon as he could. He wasn't ready to let her go by the time she got squirmy, but he did anyway. He thanked Megan and Tasha profusely as he got Ruby bundled up. Once they were in his car, Quincy asked, "Did you have a good night?"

"I did. Miss Megan and Miss Tasha were very nice to me."

"What about Sophia? Are you two getting along?"

"Sophia is my friend, Daddy," Ruby said, explaining what she felt should be clearly apparent to her father. "We started our own book club."

"Have I ever told you how glad I am that you're a reader? What are you and Sophia reading?"

"We're going to read The Babysitter's Club series. Can you take me to the library?"

"Of course, sweetheart. We can go tomorrow if you would like."

"Thank you."

"What did you have for dinner?"

"Miss Tasha made us mac and cheese. She said it was a special mac and cheese. I liked it."

"What made it special?"

"She baked it, and it had bacon in it."

"Tasha's mac sounds amazing."

"Daddy, I'm sorry, but it was better than yours."

Oof, there's an ego-killer. It's time to up my game, apparently.

"Maybe I need to get the recipe from her."

"Miss Tasha already wrote it down. I have it with my book."

Well-played, Tasha. Well-played. I guess I owe her a nice thank you.

They spent the rest of the short drive in silence.

Once in their home, Ruby said, "Sophia is so lucky."

"Why?"

"She has two mommies, and I don't have any. Daddy, do you think maybe she could share one of her mommies with me?"

Your daddy already tried, and Miss Tasha shot him down. I don't blame her. She and Megan are a great couple.

"I'm sorry, sweetheart. We can't borrow one of Sophia's mommies—Sophia would probably miss her, right? But do you remember what we've talked about? Families come in all different shapes and sizes."

"Oh." The disappointment in Ruby's voice was palpable.

"Let's get you to bed. We can read together once you are ready."

"Okay. Daddy, what about Miss Megan's friend, Mandana? She's pretty."

There's a certain irony to asking about Mandana.

"We can talk more about her tomorrow."

After Ruby was asleep, Quincy lay in his own bed where sleep evaded him.

She is pretty, beautiful, in fact. She also made it very clear that they were just doing business. Does it have to be? Well, if I catch feelings and she is just business, then I'm just setting myself up for heartbreak. No feelings, then.

Inevitably, Quincy's anxiety was overtaken by fatigue, and he fell asleep, although it was not particularly restful. When he woke in the morning, he wished he could roll over and sleep another couple of hours. With a sigh, Quincy rolled out of bed, trudged to the bathroom, and started to get ready for the day. Once he was mostly ready, he helped Ruby finish her morning routine and then walked her to school. He was thankful she didn't bring up the mommy issue.

Around eleven, Quincy signed off and went to meet Tasha's friend, Maria, for lunch. They met at an Ethiopian restaurant in NE Portland, so Quincy didn't have to go too far. Maria Rodriguez was a striking woman with long salt-and-pepper hair. She was intimidating in her pencil skirt and blazer, an effect heightened by the fact her wedges meant she was as tall as Quincy was. She didn't smile as she extended her hand for a firm handshake.

"All right, Mr. Rogers, let's get down to business."

"Of course, Ms. Rodriguez." Quincy opened the door for her, and she breezed past him.

Once seated, Maria asked, "Have you ever eaten Ethiopian before?"

"I can't say I have."

"Would you mind if I ordered for us?"

"Please, go right ahead. I don't have any dietary restrictions."

"Great." Maria rattled off a bewildering order to the server and then returned her focus to Quincy. "Tasha told me about your situation, but I want to hear it from you. You need to be completely honest with me, and I mean completely."

Quincy swallowed and began his tale in Houston after college when he first met Stacy. He talked about the booze and the drugs, the pregnancy, and getting clean. He admitted to a relapse when Ruby was barely a month old and how his mother had firmly straightened him out. Quincy had never told anyone about his relapse before. He spoke about raising Ruby, moving to Portland, the email from Stacy about custody, and his new relationship with Mandana. Maria stopped him there.

"I really don't want details about this new relationship, especially as I suspect learning more might create jeopardy for me. Let's leave it at the two of you are dating, and things might progress."

"Um, sure."

As they ate, Maria looked through her notes and peppered him with questions. Her interrogation was relentless, and Quincy soon found himself exhausted. Between Mandana last night and Maria today, he was mentally drained. Finally, the questions ended, and they concentrated on the food, which was delicious.

Quincy had never experienced anything like the texture of the injera, the soft Ethiopian flatbread used to scoop up the various meats and vegetables. His mouth felt alive with the subtle mixture of the spices.

I should bring Mandana here on one of our fake dates.

"You have a winnable case, Quincy. I think, at this point, we can be on a first-name basis, don't you?"

"Yes, Maria. When you say winnable, what do you mean?"

"Mostly, it means you have a reasonable chance of winning. You still have a chance of losing, as well. Nothing is certain until the final documents are signed."

"Any guesses about the odds of winning?"

"I'm not going to give you percentages, but with a good lawyer...well, let's just say I'm hopeful."

"I can live with 'hopeful.' Now, I need a great lawyer. Tasha said you're amazing. Would you take my case?"

"My clients are women going through divorces from husbands who are trading them in for a younger model."

"Oh." Quincy felt disappointed.

"*However,* Tasha went out of her way to contact me about your situation and urged me to help you. She and Megan like you; more importantly, they tell me your Ruby is Sophia's friend. So, I will make an exception in your case. Before you ask, yes, I primarily handle divorce cases, but those almost invariably involve family law issues."

"Thank you." Quincy felt a wave of relief wash through his body and psyche. "Thank you so much for taking this on."

"Don't thank me yet. You haven't seen my fees." Maria's expression didn't indicate any trace of humor. "We also haven't won. I promise you I will do everything I can to win."

"I appreciate your candor."

"I will tell you what I told Megan before her divorce. I am a hard-ass bitch when I need to be. Megan, of course, was far too nice, but I respect her choices."

"Good to know."

Maria then dove into the process Quincy was about to endure. She was hopeful this issue could be settled without going to court as navigating the legal process would be expensive and time-consuming, something Quincy agreed with. Maria also talked about her fees, which were eye-popping. Quincy was worried he would have to raid his 401K, but he was willing to pay any price to maintain custody of Ruby.

Despite the expense, Quincy agreed to work with Maria. She would send him documents to be signed later in the afternoon. Maria paid for lunch, writing it off as a business expense, for which Quincy was grateful. He thanked her once again for taking his case and for introducing him to Ethiopian food. Quincy headed home and resumed work until he needed to meet Ruby and walk her home from school.

As he waited outside the school for the bell to ring, Quincy kept a careful distance from Rachel, who was there for the same reason. His focus on not getting near Rachel distracted him from everything else going on, so Quincy was surprised when someone tapped him on the shoulder and said, "Boo!"

Quincy jumped and spun to see Tasha standing there laughing at him.

"Wow. I didn't expect quite so much of a reaction."

"Sorry, I was focused on not being near Rachel."

"Things are still bad between you two?"

Quincy shrugged. "Nah, it's just weird, though. Once you've seen someone naked, it's hard to interact with them as though you haven't."

"I get that, although I'm not sure I would be talking about seeing someone naked while standing in a school playground."

Quincy felt the blood racing to his cheeks. "Oh, damn. You're right. Not to change this highly embarrassing subject or anything, but how is being self-employed working out for you?"

Tasha snickered at him but answered anyway, "I'm loving it. It can be overwhelming sometimes just because I'm getting a ton of referrals. Also, I'm not as skilled at some of this stuff, which slows me down."

"Is it good money?"

"Excellent, actually. I can set my own rates, and my clients are generally happy enough to pay for what I provide."

"Good to know. If you don't mind my asking, which parts do you struggle with?"

"App designs, mostly. And some of the deeper coding for websites. I'm great with user interfaces and optimizing websites to boost sales. The underlying code is what gets me."

"Have you ever considered getting a partner to do deep-level stuff for you?"

"Right, that's what you do. Are you offering?"

"Actually, yeah."

Tasha pondered this for a minute. "You know I can't offer health care or anything, right? And I'm not sure how much business I can send you."

"Honestly, I don't really care. My job is killing me with this *return-to-the-office* bullshit, but I can deal with corporate idiocy if I have to. I'm suddenly in the position of needing extra cash. A *lot* of it."

"I'm guessing your meeting with Maria went well then."

"Yes, but she is expensive as hell. How did Megan afford her?"

"She didn't. Maria took her pro bono so long as Megan promised to be good to me. Which she is. *Very* good."

Quincy saw Tasha's eyes glaze over, and a satisfied smirk creep onto her face. He whispered, "Oh, and I'm the pervert for thinking about someone naked while on school grounds."

His remark brought Tasha back to reality quickly. "Fair. And you're my kind of pervert."

Quincy laughed.

Tasha continued, "Just to be clear, it is not all about the horizontal mambo. Megan is good to me *and for me* on a lot of levels." Tasha sighed. "I love her so much. Sometimes I feel like I'm dreaming." She shook her head. "Sorry, back to business. How about I send you an NDA and a client work order? Once you get it turned around and sent back, let me take a look at it, and we'll talk. If your work is good and we are compatible, then I'll send you more business. Either way, I'll give you fifty percent of the cut on this one."

"Sounds fair."

Tasha clapped her hands cheerily. "Awesome. If this works, then I might be able to double my business."

"Wow, really?"

"Yes. You have no idea how much coding slows me down."

Quincy grinned. "I hope I can help. Thank you, Tasha."

The bell rang a few seconds later, interrupting their discussion as they were suddenly waist-deep in a wave of running children. The air was suddenly filled with a cacophony of parents calling for kids and the high-pitched chatter of the kids themselves.

Ruby and Sophia held hands as they ran up to Quincy and Tasha.

"Mama Tasha, Ruby said she was going to the library today. Can I go with her?"

"Of course, munchkin."

"Tasha, if you want, I'm happy to watch the girls and take them to the library after I'm done with work. I can drop Sophia off afterward."

"Sophia, would you like to spend the afternoon with Mister Quincy?"

"Yes, Mama Tasha!"

Quincy checked in with Ruby. "Sweetheart, is Sophia coming over okay with you?"

"Yes, Daddy."

"All right, it's settled then. I'll bring Sophia by later then."

"Sounds great—" Tasha suddenly seemed to have a weak moment but recovered immediately. "Um, it would be terrific if you texted, or called, or maybe both when you are on your way." Tasha's voice was taking on a breathless quality.

Quincy gave her a lascivious grin. "I can definitely provide advance notice. Have fun. Okay, young ladies, let's go."

They all waved to Tasha as they set off. Once home, the girls parked themselves on the couch with their books, and Dolly Purrton joined them. The two girls idly petted the cat as they read, and all three seemed happy.

After Quincy was off work, he walked the two girls over to the library. He kept an eye on them as they meandered through the children's section. They each had a notebook and were taking notes of some sort. After about thirty minutes, Quincy checked in with them. Their notes were book ideas for their new book club, which impressed Quincy. The girls each had a couple of books to check out, and then they would be ready to go.

Before leaving the library, Quincy diligently texted and called Tasha, getting a text reply simply saying, "Thanks." Sophia had her keys so they could get into the building. As the lock was turning on the apartment door, the door opened suddenly, and a very disheveled and sweaty Tasha stood there, panting. Behind her, an equally disheveled Megan tugged at her shirt.

"I have returned Sophia, safe and sound, as promised. The girls had a great time at the library." Quincy lowered his voice to a whisper and leaned into Tasha's ear. "Your shirt is on inside out."

Chapter 8

Ride Like the Wind

Saxon

Mandana's day was packed solid with preparations for starting a new business. She oscillated back and forth between giddy excitement and intense frustration all day long. Her agent identified a likely property down in the Lloyd district. The property had been empty for a couple of years, which was not a great sign; however, if the Lloyd Center Mall was ever repurposed or replaced, it could be an incredible location. Mandana had the money to survive over a few lean years if needed, so she wasn't too worried.

She hired a lawyer based on a recommendation from Megan and Tasha's friend, who helped her navigate the pitfalls of starting a business. The immense number of steps needed to start a business was staggering: miles of paperwork, a business plan to write, contractors to hire for the necessary renovations to keep the cats safe. The process was daunting, to say the least.

Mandana decided to step down to part-time at the bar, working only Fridays and Saturdays starting the following week. She made the bulk of her money on those nights anyway, and this freed up time for her to work on the business.

And go out on more fake dates with Quincy. Why am I thinking of him right now? Speak of the devil; he's calling me.

"Hi, Que Tee."

"I'm sorry, what?"

"Um, it's a nickname. Your name starts with 'Q,' so I came up with Que Tee."

"Alrighty, then. I'm not sure how I feel about it, but I guess there are worse nicknames to have."

The nickname was a terrible idea. Why did I blurt out something so stupid? Whatever, it's not like we're really dating anyway.

Quincy continued, "My middle name is Thomas, so it actually works." He grunted, "I wonder if my parents thought of nicknames when they named me."

"I'm glad it works, and you don't hate it."

"I'll get used to it. Before you distracted me, I was calling to ask you out on another date. Maybe Monday or Tuesday since those are your days off?"

"I'm about to have more availability after this weekend, but Monday works fine for me."

"Awesome, have you ever tried Ethiopian?"

"Nope, but I'll give it a shot."

"Would you prefer to meet there, or should I pick you up?"

"Let's decide later. I gotta go. Megan's yoga class starts soon."

"Okay, have fun. Hopefully, she's not too tired."

"Bye."

Why would she be too tired for yoga?

Mandana made it to the class just in time. She got in a great workout, and the poses helped relieve the stress of the day. After class, she sidled up to Megan, who drank deeply from her water bottle. "Hi, great class as always."

"Hi, yourself. Thank you. How are you feeling?"

"So good. I really needed your class to center myself. By the way, why did Quincy suggest you might be too tired for yoga tonight?"

Megan choked on her water, face flushing rapidly.

"Are you okay?"

"Yeah—" Megan punctuated her pause with another cough, waving away the concerned looks around the room. "Let me meet you outside in five, alright?"

Mildly concerned, Mandana packed up her gear and loitered at the entrance. When Megan arrived, Mandana felt herself quickly dragged down the street. Once safely out of range of any snooping ears, Megan told her, "Quincy was watching the girls after school, and he took them to the library."

"Uh-huh."

"So, when I got home, Tasha was wearing stockings."

"Uh-huh."

Megan looked hungry as she half purred, half growled. "*Just stockings.*"

"Oh…"

"Yeah. I'd like to say we made sweet love, but we didn't. We fucked each other silly. For the second time in three days. We have this double-ended—" Even in the dim light on the sidewalk, Mandana could see Megan's blush. "I'm sorry, I'm spilling way too much information."

"You go, girl. Get some and be proud of it." Mandana raised her hand for a high five, which Megan sheepishly slapped.

"I kinda am. Proud of it, I mean. I'd never been with a woman before Tasha, and our sex is amazing. Maybe it is because we already had a deep emotional bond. Can I tell you another thing I probably shouldn't?"

"Only if you want to. Trust me, there's nothing you can say that will shock me more than the stuff I hear at the bar."

"I discovered that I love to lie down and have Tasha climb on top of me and fuck my face. I'm not sure what about having her ride my face does it for me, but I love it. Maybe it's because I can play with myself while she's doing it."

"Have you cum at the same time doing this?"

"We did today."

"Damn, you two are so hot, Megan. I gotta try face riding the next time I can get a guy in bed."

"It can't be hard to get one." Megan gave her an admiring look. "You're super hot."

"Thank you. Honestly, it's not hard to get a guy in the sack. I'm just over the casual thing and definitely over bar hook-ups. If I'm going to get a guy in bed, I want him to actually care about my pleasure."

Megan grinned deviously. "I can think of one guy who would care about pleasing you..."

"I'm not going there, Megan. Strictly business. Mixing in sex would make things complicated."

"Complicated can be fun...anyway, want to come over for dinner? Tasha made a fresh batch of chili. Sophia should be in bed so we can do the girl chat thing."

"Sure. Sounds fun, at least for a little bit. I know you have to get up for work in the morning."

"Great. We want to hear about how the whole cat cafe thing is going."

"Ugh, I love it and hate it at the same time..."

Chapter 9

Round and Round

Ratt

On Wednesday morning, Quincy and Tasha met as they were dropping off their respective kids. "Good morning, Tasha. I'm sorry it took me so long to finish working on the app for you."

"Oh, no problem at all, Que Tee."

Quincy flinched.

Tasha added, "Is Que Tee not a thing now?"

"Honestly, I'm still getting used to the idea of Mandana calling me a nickname. If every beautiful woman in Portland starts using that nickname, then either my ego will explode, or I'll have to hide myself in embarrassment."

"Mmm, hiding your handsome face would be a shame, tiger," Tasha purred at him, gently stroking her fingertips across his biceps.

A new voice asked, "What would be a shame?"

Quincy turned his head to see Rachel standing on the other side of him from Tasha.

Oh no. I can't deal with Rachel right now.

Tasha looked directly at Rachel and put an arm around Quincy's waist as she whispered provocatively, "My wife and I were hoping to bring this stud home for another threesome."

Rachel blanched and fled.

Quincy looked at Tasha and hissed, "What the hell?"

Tasha giggled. "I saw her coming over here, looking all jealous at us while we were talking. Now I've given her something to think about when she goes home to Brad."

Quincy was puzzled. "I am pretty sure her husband is named Simon."

She shrugged. "Meh. When I think of a boring, lights-off, missionary sex-only husband, somehow the name Brad always comes to mind. Anyway, she dumped you, and now she'll wonder what kind of sex god she let slip away."

"Wow, you're evil, Tasha, but I kinda like it."

He observed Tasha quickly transition from sex kitten to businesswoman in the blink of an eye. "You did great work on the app.

I like how it seamlessly communicates with their website and their inventory software. Seriously, it would have taken me all day to do half as good of a job."

Quincy beamed. "Thank you. I appreciate it. Can you work with what I've done?"

"I think so. I'm going to overlay the user interface this morning. If it goes as well as I think it will, can I send you more work?"

"Yes, definitely. I hate to take more time away from Ruby, especially right now, but I need the money."

"Speaking of Ruby, do you want me to watch them today? Maybe we could even switch off. Like every other day."

"Provided the girls are fine with switching, then I like that idea. Did you need me to watch Sophia on Sunday morning? You know, for your nude yoga class. I could watch her all day Sunday if you need me to."

"Sunday morning is a great idea," Tasha said excitedly. She looked upward, accessing her memory. "Actually, we were thinking of taking Sophia to the Zoo in the afternoon on Sunday. Would you and Ruby like to join us?"

"We would like that a lot. Thank you."

"You're welcome."

"Since we are already planning these things out, can you all watch Ruby on Monday night?"

Tasha's eyes danced with interest. "Date night with Mandana?"

"Yes."

"*Oh*," she purred. "How is dating going?" She added air quotes for "dating."

"For fake dating? Great, I guess. We are establishing a dating history, so all of this looks legitimate."

"Ugh. You're so boring and business-like," Tasha pouted. "You'll still have a really fast engagement."

"And how long was it for you and Megan?"

"A couple of weeks, maybe."

"See, you are inspiring us."

"Yeah, but we had history."

Quincy whispered conspiratorially, "True, but with Mandana and I, when you fake know, you fake know."

Tasha laughed at his silliness. "All right, I'm gonna head out. I'll be in touch later."

"Me too. I'll text Ruby about the afternoon."

"Perfect. Bye now."

Quincy got home and dove immediately into work. His day was a long series of band-aid projects, trying to somehow make incompatible software work together. Once he punched all of his job tickets, he turned to more freelance work from Tasha. This work was at least fun, and so long as his bosses didn't know he was doing it, then he was fine.

Yet another thing returning to the office will ruin. I think it's time to get my resume out there. I'm not going back to a cubicle.

Quincy took a break from freelance work to update his resume, which he posted on some boards he knew were frequented by headhunters. He got back to work and finished a project for Tasha. She was effusive in her praise and added an invite to join them for dinner after work. Quincy wasn't one to pass up a home-cooked meal.

As Tasha led him toward her apartment, he could smell something fabulous permeating the hallway. Once inside, the scent of whatever Megan was preparing delighted his nostrils. He asked, "What are you making?"

Megan answered, "Hi, Que Tee. I'm making chicken makhani for dinner along with aloo palak. Also known as butter chicken and creamed spinach. The girls are making naan."

"I love naan. Ruby, you made it?"

"Yes, Daddy. Miss Megan has been teaching me how to cook."

"Wow, really?" He looked at Megan. "You didn't—"

Megan waved away his concern. "Hush, it's fine. Tasha and I have been teaching Sophia how to cook, so it's easy to include Ruby in the lessons as well. She has good instincts. Both girls do."

Tasha clapped her hands. "All right, angels. Please set the table for us. Quincy, can you take a look at something for me?"

"Sure," he said, following Tasha. They took a few minutes to go over some technical challenges which would have taken much more time to resolve remotely. "Thanks, Que Tee. That was easy. I'm not sending you too much work, am I?"

"Y'all are killing me with the new nickname. No, the workload is fine."

"Awesome. Tell me if it gets to be too much."

"I will."

Tasha groaned hungrily. "Good, now let's eat. I've had to smell this *forever*."

The meal was excellent, and the girls looked incredibly pleased whenever someone ate their naan.

"Megan, girls, this is so tasty."

"Thank you."

"I dated an Indian girl in college, and this is almost as good as her mom's cooking."

Megan blushed. "Wow. That's quite the compliment. I do my best. I've taken some online cooking courses. I hope to take some in-person ones since I'm now settled in Portland."

"Your best is already quite good, but I respect the dedication to improvement."

Tasha jumped into the conversation, adding, "What happened with the Indian girl you dated in college?"

Quincy sighed. "I was...a distraction. Her parents were very nice to me, but they subtly made it quite clear I would not be a permanent part of their daughter's life. She ended up marrying an Indian guy they found for her."

"That's rough."

"Eh, it's all right. We had chemistry but no spark."

Quincy noticed Ruby looking at him expectantly. "You look like you are excited to tell me something."

"Daddy, I picked my roller derby name. I want to be Book Wyrm, spelled with a 'y.'"

"Your roller derby name? I think Tasha mentioned something about roller derby to me. What is it?"

"It's this amazing sport, and girls like me play it. Sophia has been showing me videos. It looks super fun, Daddy."

"Huh. And you want to play this sport?"

"Yes. Sophia is going to tryouts on Saturday. Can I go, too?"

"Really? You've never wanted to play any sports before."

Ruby started bouncing in her chair. "This one is different. Please?"

"I'd like to see some of these videos first, okay?"

"We can show you after dinner!"

"I'll take a look. No promises, though."

"Okay."

Turning to Megan and Tasha, Quincy asked, "What am I about to get myself into?"

Megan answered, "I'm not entirely sure from a time perspective, but I gotta say, the sport itself is a lot of fun. I'm actually thinking of joining their adult recreational league."

"Oh, wow. So adults and kids can play this."

"Not at the same time, obviously, but yes. We've talked with some skaters and their parents after the bouts, and everyone seems very welcoming."

"You're not worried about Sophia getting hurt?"

Megan nodded. "Of course I am. There are limited contact rules at their age, and there are lots of referees to keep the game under control and a medical team if something happens. It's not one hundred percent safe, and injuries do happen, but I feel better about this than I would in some other sports."

"Huh. What about you, Tasha?"

"I love watching this. It's a very empowering sport and appeals to kids who may not fit into traditional sports options." Tasha sighed. "I blew out my knee in college playing soccer, but Megan here keeps bugging me to get checked out. She wants to skate with me." Megan blushed.

"Ruby said there are tryouts this weekend?"

"It's a boot camp, actually. Anyone who joins needs to go through the boot camp and then follow-up training. You must meet certain criteria before being deemed safe to skate, including the ability to fall safely."

Quincy nodded, impressed. "Okay, so this is a serious thing, then."

"Very serious. The adult travel team for the Rose City Rollers is the current defending world champion."

"Wow, really?"

"Yes, and unlike most sports in the U.S., this is a genuine world championship with teams from around the globe competing."

Quincy snickered at Tasha's statement because he knew it was true.

"Well, I'm mostly sold. I still want to watch these videos, though."

After dinner and watching some roller derby videos, Quincy agreed to sign Ruby up for the boot camp. Ruby and Sophia were very excited to go to the boot camp together. Before they left, Quincy asked Ruby if she liked spending the afternoons with Sophia every day, which Ruby affirmed.

"Ruby likes this switch-off afternoons thing. Do you want me to watch Sophia tomorrow afternoon?" Quincy couldn't help but see the lustful look passing between Megan and Tasha. "You don't have to say anything. I'll take your look as a 'Yes' then."

The two women laughed. Megan responded, "Sound's perfect, and then we can watch Ruby on Friday."

"Great. I will text and call before I come over tomorrow." Quincy gave them a knowing wink.

Chapter 10
The Zoo

Scorpions

Exhaustion was hitting Mandana hard by the end of her Saturday night shift. A nap in the afternoon helped, but she was still feeling the strain of working a full week in the evening along with so much work on the new business. She was asleep only moments after her head hit her pillow, sleeping soundly until her alarm pierced the dark veil of slumber. Mandana rose with a mild curse, stumbling toward the shower. One shower and one coffee later, she felt ready to meet Megan and Tasha for another session of nude yoga.

As the trio returned to Megan and Tasha's place, Mandana reveled in the feelings left over from the class.

"Thank you for being willing to do this with me again. Something about not wearing clothes makes me feel connected and free. I can't remember ever feeling like this before."

Tasha chortled, "Trust me, it is our pleasure."

"Are you ever not horny?"

While Tasha pondered Mandana's question, Megan answered for her, "Trust me, Tasha is always horny." Addressing Tasha, Megan continued, "I don't mind, my love. You make me feel very desirable.

"You two are unbelievably cute. It's inspiring."

"For the record, I'm not *always* horny. Megan inspires me on many levels—" Tasha sighed contentedly. "She's the love of my life. I hope you find a life partner someday, Mandana. Speaking of, where is Quincy taking you on Monday?"

Mandana groaned. "Don't start, Tasha. Quincy and I have agreed there will be no feelings and no strings. Anyway, he's taking me out for Ethiopian food."

"Oh, nice. You have to tell us how it is," Megan gushed. "There's so much good food in this city. I love it."

Tasha chimed in. "We should do a potluck. Next Sunday, maybe. Would you come for a potluck, Mandana, and maybe bring something?"

"Well—"

"Say yes. Megan is an amazing cook."

"You are, too, Tasha."

"—yes, I would love to. I am already thinking of a couple of incredible Persian dishes I could make."

"That's so exciting."

Tasha's energy was infectious, and Mandana couldn't help but grin.

"I'm not working Sunday nights anymore, either, so I can stay as long as I want."

Tasha clapped her hands. "You must be relieved, Mandana. Oh, do you want to come to the Zoo with us this afternoon?

"I can't remember the last time I went to a zoo. I must have been a kid. I've got nothing else going on, so I'll go with you."

"Great. Do you need to change?"

The palpable horniness in Megan's voice as she asked her question strongly suggested Mandana's only answer needed to be 'Yes.'

"Perfect. How about we pick you up in, say, two hours?"

"I'll see you horndogs then."

Two hours later, Mandana climbed into Megan's car.

"Um, where's Sophia?"

Megan answered breezily, "We're meeting her there."

They tricked me because I know exactly who is bringing Sophia. I was too distracted by their horniness to see the setup coming. Well played, Megan and Tasha. Well-played.

"Oh, and who will be bringing her to the Zoo?" Mandana asked, knowing what the answer would be.

Megan at least had the decency to blush at their subterfuge as she whispered guiltily, "Quincy."

Just as I suspected, the trap is sprung.

"You two aren't trying to set us up for real, are you?"

"Of course not. We just thought this would be a fun outing for everyone."

Megan is a terrible liar. I love her for trying, but wow, she has no poker face.

"Uh-huh."

Megan kept talking, "I'm sure you will have a great time. It's not like we plan to leave you alone with Quincy."

They are definitely planning to leave me alone with Quincy.

Mandana responded sardonically, "You definitely wouldn't ditch the two of us. I'm sure the six of us will have a great time together. All together in the same places."

"Exactly. See, it will be fun."

I suppose there are worse things in life than spending time with a handsome man, especially since I'm already fake-dating him.

When they arrived, Quincy and the two girls were waiting for them. Sophia ran and hugged her moms. Once everyone was inside, Megan asked where they should go first. Ruby responded immediately, saying, "We want to see the beavers!"

Megan and Tasha were almost giggling, too hard to agree, but somehow managed to start walking in the right direction. Trailing behind, Quincy sidled up to Mandana and whispered, "Do you ever get sick of how in love they are?"

"Nope."

Quincy grinned, "Me either."

Megan and Tasha walked slightly ahead, each holding one of Sophia's hands. Mandana walked behind them, absently looking around, when she felt a touch on her hand. Looking down, she could see it was Ruby, who was already holding one of Quincy's hands. The girl's smile was irresistible. With an imperceptible sigh at potentially breaking Quincy's rule, Mandana wordlessly held Ruby's hand. The girl's smile somehow grew more prominent, and Mandana smiled back. Raising her head, she saw Quincy give her an apologetic shrug.

"Mandana, have you ever played roller derby?"

"No, Ruby, I haven't. I've never seen it, actually."

"It's so much fun. Daddy is letting me play. Sophia and I tried it out yesterday. I already picked out my derby name. Wanna know what it is?"

"What is it?"

"My name is Book Wyrm. Spelled with a 'y' like dragons."

"*Wow.* You picked an awesome name. I like it."

Quincy chortled. "It suits her, too. She is a voracious reader."

"It's good you like reading at your age, Book Wyrm."

"You are beautiful! Like a queen, but one of the nice ones."

"Thank you. You're adorable. You are also very pretty."

"Thank you. Daddy thinks you are pretty, too." Quincy made a choking sound.

"Oh, he does, does he?"

Ruby changed the subject exuberantly, "Do you like flowers?"

Mandana nodded. "Yes."

Ruby turned to her father. "Daddy, you should give Miss Mandana flowers on your date tomorrow."

I have no idea what to do with her stream of consciousness; clearly, Quincy doesn't either.

"Sophia is going to show me how to make lasagna for dinner tomorrow while you are on your date."

"Wow, you'll be a better cook than me."

I think Quincy's brain might be broken. Maybe I should ask her to spill more of her dad's secrets. It's probably best if I don't.

"Beavers!" Suddenly, Ruby was off and running, joining Sophia in excitedly observing the semi-aquatic mammals.

"Are you okay?"

Quincy shook himself a bit before answering, "Sorry. Eight-year-olds don't have much of a filter."

"It's quite all right. She's charming."

He looked wistfully at his daughter, "She is amazing. I'm not sure how I got so lucky."

He truly loves her. It's difficult to wrap my mind around the idea of loving someone so much to be willing to fake dating a complete stranger to boost his chance to keep custody of her. She's a lucky kid.

The two girls bounced from exhibit to exhibit with the boundless energy of eight-year-olds, with the adults trailing along as best they could. Mandana found herself enraptured by the river otters, watching their lithe forms glide effortlessly through the water. When she looked up, Quincy was the only one there.

"Where are the girls?"

"They're with Megan and Tasha. Um, Tasha insisted I stay with you."

And the trap closes.

"You know this is a setup, right?"

Quincy's eyes danced in wild panic. "What? Really?"

He is either a phenomenal actor or simply clueless. The Oscar for Best Actor in a Romantic Comedy goes to...Quincy Rogers. Please tell me I'm not in a rom-com. If Lacey Chabert walks around the next corner, I am out of here.

"Yes, really. Did they tell you I was coming today?"

"No."

"And Tasha just told you to wait for me rather than go with your own daughter?"

"Yeah. Oh..."

Wow, he is incredibly clueless sometimes. Good thing he's hot. Why did he have to be hot, a caring father, and a nice guy?

"Figured it out now?"

Quincy sputtered, "Yes. But we told them it was all fake, right?"

"Multiple times. They're a couple, and they have two single friends. It's like a compulsion; they can't help themselves, and they have to try to set us up."

"We're not together, though. We made our deal. We told them."

"It's okay. We'll just find them and the girls."

"What if they are filling Ruby's head with this? She can't get attached."

"It will be fine. She's a smart kid."

Desperation crept into his voice. "No, you don't understand—"

"Excuse me?"

"No offense," Quincy stammered. "A few nights ago, Ruby told me how lucky she thought Sophia was because Sophia had two mommies. She asked if she could share one of Sophia's mommies."

Mandana snickered, "Too bad Tasha shot you down."

Quincy's shoulders slumped as he sighed. "Of course, she told you." Getting serious, he continued, "If Ruby thinks we are real, and then we end it, you know because it's all fake, then she'll get hurt."

We're swimming in some deep water right now. It explains why he is so upset.

"Hey, Quincy. I like Ruby, and I think she is a great kid. I like you, too, and you are obviously a very caring and devoted father—" *And surprisingly hot. Why am I thinking this? Focus, Mandana.* "—and I don't want to hurt either of you." *What the hell does that even mean?* "We will figure this out, Quincy. Trust me."

Is he crying right now? Oh, and we're hugging. Shit, he's strong.. .and gentle. Nice muscles. And he's emotionally vulnerable and not caught up in macho bullshit about not showing his feelings. Fuck, why am I getting wet? Oh yeah, a hot guy who pushes all the right buttons is in my arms. And I'm in his arms. Dammit, I'm going to be wetter than the beaver pond if this keeps up. Mmmm, maybe he could put his log in my beaver pond. Get a grip, Mandana. No sex was the deal. Plus, I don't want to be a mom. Although, if I were going to be a mom, Ruby would be...nope, shut those thoughts down, Mandana. No attachments...I wonder what Quincy's attachment feels like.

Mandana's mental struggle was eased as Quincy broke their embrace. He wiped his eyes and said, "I'm sorry. I feel like I crossed a line there. It's just—"

"Shhh, it's okay. Thank you for being vulnerable. Hugs are wonderful. Sometimes, people just need to hug one another."

"Thanks for being so understanding, Mandana."

"Our society often stigmatizes physical contact, especially for men. It's unfortunate because physical connection is often vital."

"You are absolutely correct."

"See, agreeing with me shows you are a smart man." Mandana grinned and held out her hand. "Now, let's go find our meddling friends and the girls."

Chapter 11

Can't Fight This Feeling

REO Speedwagon

Later that night, Quincy imagined he could still feel the warmth of Mandana's hand in his. Guilt crept into his mind, and he tried to banish those memories, but they persisted.

I'm not supposed to enjoy the feel of her skin. It's definitely wrong to remember how soft her hands were in some places but calloused in others. I shouldn't be missing the strength of her grip or the comfort I felt. She held my hand like a friend and nothing more. Just friends.

Sleep found him eventually, and he drifted off into pleasant slumber. In the morning, he walked Ruby to school and chatted with Tasha. Usually, it would be his day to watch the girls, but she insisted on picking them up today so he could prepare for his fake date with Mandana. He countered with an offer to watch the girls the next day and also take them to their Wednesday derby skills practice. Tasha thought this was a fair trade. As he walked away, Quincy noted how Rachel kept very far away from them.

As the day progressed, Quincy became increasingly nervous about the upcoming not-date. Somehow, after crying in Mandana's arms and holding her hand, this date seemed somewhat less fake.

I can't let Mandana know I'm catching feelings. She was very clear about the no emotions thing, and I can't afford to blow this. She felt good. In retrospect, really, really good. Her arms were strong and firm, yet comforting. Her hair smelled almost intoxicating, too. Nice shoulders, firm but not too hard. Okay, I need to stop.

Mandana offered to pick him up because it made the most sense. He decided on khakis and a nice sweater for their date and met her at the appointed time. As he clambered into her Audi, his breath caught. Mandana was wearing a long, flowing red sleeveless dress, which showed off her arm tattoos to great effect. She had the dress pulled up to keep her feet free, exposing knee-high black boots.

Holy shit. She looks incredibly hot.

"Hi. Thank you for picking me up."

"Hey, and you are welcome."

"You look gorgeous."

"Thank you. You clean up nicely, too," Mandana responded neutrally.

Once at the restaurant, Quincy felt the lighting was dimmer and more intimate than when he was there with Maria for lunch. It took a while to decide what to order, as neither of them was familiar with what they were about to get. They agreed on what was essentially a sharing plate of a lot of different options. Once the order was in, Quincy asked, "How was your day?"

"Ugh. Super busy. Setting up a new business is a lot of work. Meetings and phone calls all day. I think I'm insane to be doing this."

"I'm not sure I would be able to do it, so I respect your drive and ambition."

"Thanks." She sounded weary.

"Have you decided on a name yet?"

"The Purrsian Paradise."

Quincy guffawed, "Wow, really?"

"What? You came up with it." There was a hint of indignation in her voice.

"I know. I never expected you actually to use it, but I'm proud you did."

"I honestly didn't expect to use it, either, but it grew on me."

"I'm glad I could help. Can you tell me about your vision for the cat cafe?"

"Sure. Customers would enter through the main door with the counter right in front of them. To one side would be a glass wall with a door, and the cats are beyond the glass. Once inside, customers would order drinks and baked goods. I'm trying to line up some bakeries to provide those. After customers order, they can sit at a counter outside of the cat room if they want or go in. An employee would let them in because we must ensure the cats stay inside. Once in the cat room, there will be different seating options, ranging from standard tables and chairs to high boys, but what I'm most excited about are the low benches and cushions for Persian-style seating."

"Your concept sounds like fun."

"Yes, it will be. The decor will be Persian, of course. Finally, there will be a back room where the cats live. They will be able to go in and out as they please. I'm working with local shelters, so at least some cats will be adoptable."

"Even better. Imagine going and getting coffee and a muffin and coming home with a cat. Ruby would love to see it. Well, she would drink hot chocolate instead of coffee. You'll have hot chocolate, right?"

Mandana chuckled, "Slow down. Yes, we will definitely have hot chocolate. It seems you really like this concept."

"I absolutely love it. I'll be there every weekend."

Mandana's chuckle evolved into a full-blown laugh. "Well, at least I will have one regular customer."

"Seriously, though, I absolutely think this will be a hit. You must be excited."

"Excited is one word. There's also anxious, terrified, and over-whelmed."

Quincy nodded sagely. "I get your concerns. It's a risky endeavor, and those feelings are completely valid. On the plus side, you seem very smart and business savvy, and all those years as a bartender mean you know customer service inside and out."

"I appreciate your confidence in me. What about you? How was your day?"

"Let me preface my response by saying I have been working from home for years, and it's been amazing. I get my work done, my reviews have been stellar, and it allows me to take care of Ruby."

Mandana nodded in response.

"My company has been pushing people to return to the office since before the pandemic ended, and they've been ramping up the pressure, especially in the last year."

"Uh oh, I think I see where this is going."

"Yep. So today, I got a directive to be back in the office next Monday, so I have no excuses. Well, calling out sick is valid, but I have to go back no matter what."

"Have they said why?"

"Supposedly, we all work better when we are together, which is mostly bullshit. Maybe some people, but not me. I'm buried in code all day. No part of my job works better in the office. Personally, I think it's either because they have empty office space they are locked into paying for, or maybe it's because all the managers need people to manage, or else someone might figure out they don't actually do anything."

"I'm going to go with both answers. Speaking of being buried in code, what is it you do all day?"

"Basically, my company purchases a lot of software for various purposes. More often than not, each piece of software is incompatible with at least one other piece of software. My job is to find some way to make everything work together."

"So, you're a duct taper?"

"Holy shit, you read *Bullshit Jobs*, too?"

"Yes, it's one of my favorite books. Every time my parents bug me about being a bartender instead of working a corporate job, I think about *Bullshit Jobs,* and suddenly I'm thrilled to be a bartender."

"Well, now you're a small business owner."

"Almost. So, go on."

"Oh, right. I'm supposed to go back to the office next week, and I'm not going to do it. I put my resume out last week and got three hits from headhunters today."

"Nice. What are you going to do?"

"I'm trying to decide. I feel like I have two options. For the first option, I could negotiate a deal with my current company for guaranteed remote work, better pay, and reduced hours, all of which I'm getting from these other offers. For the second option, I could simply take one of their offers."

"Here's a fun thought. You could take one of those offers, and if the workload is light, take another one and get twice the money."

"Intriguing thought. It sounds tempting but risky. Plus, if I have a super light workload, I think I would rather spend more time with Ruby or do freelance work from Tasha."

"Probably a better choice. I don't have kids, so that didn't occur to me."

"And you really don't want kids? I always hear how motherhood is such a gift."

"I don't. For some, motherhood is a gift, and that's great. But a lot of people I've talked to, while they love their kids, aren't as enthusiastic about the whole carrying a bowling ball, forcing it out, and then nursing thing. Let me turn the question around: would you do it again?"

"Oh, I never thought about it." Quincy pondered the question silently for a minute. "Would I do it again? Yes. Conditionally."

"How so?"

"You're right; sleepless nights and changing diapers are awful. I would do it again if I was with someone and they wanted a child, but otherwise, I would not choose to go through all of the insomnia and awful smells again."

"What about someone with kids who wanted another one?"

"I would have to think long and hard before deciding."

"Long and hard..." Mandana giggled wickedly.

"Are Megan and Tasha rubbing off on you? Wait, don't answer." Mandana just kept giggling.

Quincy was saved from any further verbal *faux pas* by the arrival of dinner. The meal smelled fantastic, and Mandana was finally able to contain her giggles as she surveyed the spicy goodness before them. "So, we just rip off some of this bread and scoop up what we want to eat?"

"Exactly. It's like naan but with a completely different taste and texture. The injera acts kind of like a sponge, too."

"It looks so good." Mandana quickly dug in while Quincy indecisively surveyed the options.

"Oh my God, you've got to try this." Quincy glanced up to see Mandana holding out a piece of injera dripping with meat and spices. Without thinking, he leaned forward and bit into it, savoring the rush of the spices and the tactile sensation of the injera. He closed his eyes and concentrated on the sensations in his mouth.

"Wow, that is amazing—" Mandana was staring at him across the table.

Uh oh, she looks pissed.

"What. The. *Fuck*. Quincy?"

"What did...oh..."

I ate right off of her fingers.

"I'm really sorry."

I don't think I'm actually sorry. In retrospect, I liked it.

"Whatever, it's fine." Mandana started eating again.

The universal code for 'It is one hundred percent not fine.'

After taking a couple of bites himself, Quincy tentatively said, "This is good; you should try it," while pointing at something that looked like lentils.

Mandana gave him a flat look.

"What? I'm really sorry." Quincy felt panic rising in his guts.

She deliberately placed her hands in her lap and leaned forward.

"Do you want me to?"

Her silent glare was searing.

Here goes nothing.

Quincy tore off some injera and dipped it into the lentils, carefully raising it toward Mandana's lips. As the morsel approached, she opened her mouth. He delicately placed it on her tongue, and then his fingers retreated, narrowly avoiding the snap of her teeth. Quincy watched as she closed her eyes and savored the bite. She swallowed and opened her eyes. Those walnut brown irises danced with mischief, and a devilish grin spread across her lips. Silently, Mandana pushed her chair back and rose, those mesmerizing eyes capturing his gaze. Her dress swished as she stepped to the side, pushed her chair in, and then pulled out the chair adjacent to his. She sat down, and only the corner of the table was between them. Mandana broke their eye contact to reach down and collect another morsel of food. In agonizing silence, she once again trapped his vision as her hand moved implacably toward his mouth. Quincy's jaw opened, accepting her proffered food. Her fingers lingered as he slowly brought his teeth together, leaving a gentle caress on his lips as they slowly withdrew.

His eyes closed as he once again savored the food in his mouth. At the same time, Quincy felt the heat of his blood and the pounding of his heart. He was all too conscious of the strain in his pants.

That was, without question, the sexiest experience of my entire life. I'm still not sure if she is angry with me or not, but it was worth it.

When he opened his eyes again, Mandana's burning gaze was fixed upon him, but he didn't detect the earlier anger. Her hands were folded neatly in her lap. Taking the silent hint, Quincy selected something from the platter and once again brought it to Mandana's lips. This time, he let his own fingers linger, and he felt her tongue slide across his fingertips as he withdrew, her lips softly bidding his fingers farewell.

They continued like this for the rest of dinner, feeding each other sensuously in silence. Quincy opened his mouth once to speak but was immediately silenced by a glare from Mandana.

I still have no idea what is happening, but I am immensely turned on right now. I think I would be perfectly content if this dinner never ended.

Unfortunately for Quincy, dinner inevitably concluded. Their silence lingered as if speaking would somehow break this spell. Quincy paid the check, and the pair walked to the door. The hush continued until they reached Quincy's apartment. As he reached for the door handle, Mandana whispered, "Thank you for dinner."

Quincy looked back at her, "You are welcome."

"Let's do this again sometime."

"Definitely. Good night, Mandana."

"Good night, Quincy."

He walked from her car to his and then drove for a short time to Megan and Tasha's place to pick up Ruby.

Chapter 12

It's Not Love

Dokken

Megan touched Mandana's arm at the end of the Tuesday night yoga class. "Hey, are you all right?"

Shaking her head as if to clear the cobwebs in her brain, Mandana answered, "Yeah, I'm fine. Just distracted."

"Do you want to talk about it?"

Mandana nodded shyly. "Would you mind if I invite myself over for tea?"

"Not at all. I'll text Tasha and have her start boiling water. I'll see you outside in a couple of minutes."

A short while later, the three women were seated around the table with steaming mugs of tea.

Tasha's patience cracked first. "Okay, girl. Quincy looked like his brain got run over by a train last night. What the hell happened at dinner? Spill."

Mandana's fingers silently traced her mug's designs before she quietly said, "I think I messed up last night." She paused.

As the silent pause extended, Megan placed a calming hand on Tasha's arm. "How?"

Mandana felt guilt and shame creeping onto her face. "It's hard to explain. The best description I can think of is that we had food sex."

Tasha exclaimed, "I have no idea what food sex means, but I want to know more."

Megan said gently, "I'm sure you do, love. I'm curious as well. Mandana, maybe start from the beginning."

"Sure, we had a very nice conversation about the cat cafe and his job issues—"

"Job issues?" Tasha sounded concerned.

"The job part is Quincy's story to tell. Back to last night. The food arrived on this big platter with the injera and a sampling of all of these amazing dishes. I tried one of them. Lamb something, I forget. Anyway, I told Quincy he should try it and held out some of it for him to try. Instead of just taking it out of my hand like a normal person, he bit it off of my fingers."

"Like, bit your fingers, or—"

"Not quite, but essentially, it was like I fed him."

Tasha grimaced. "Huh. Weird. How did you feel?"

"It was strange. I felt angry, upset, turned on, maybe degraded, maybe empowered. All at once."

Megan quietly said, "That is a lot."

"It was. Quincy quickly figured out I was pissed. He apologized, but his words didn't make me feel better. Then, he awkwardly tried to be positive and pointed out a different item, which he said looked good. Next, he suggested I try it." Mandana paused again, her mind drifting back to the previous night.

Tasha was ready to explode with anticipation. "And then what?"

"Right, sorry. I put my hands in my lap and kept them there. Quincy put some of it on injera and fed it to me."

Megan shuddered and groaned. "So fucking hot. Did you suck his fingers or something?"

"No, I actually nearly bit them off. I was still pretty pissed. But between the food, the lighting, and him feeding me...I don't know. It's like something deep inside me took over. I changed seats, so I was next to him instead of across from him."

"What did you say?"

"Nothing. I said absolutely nothing."

Tasha groaned, "Goddess, you're so fucking hot."

"Then, I took another helping of food and fed it to Quincy, but this time slowly and sensuously."

"Please tell me he did the same."

"Oh, he did, except I sucked his fingers a bit."

"I am so fucking wet right now. Megan…"

Megan's voice sounded tense. "Me too, Tasha. I'll take care of you, my love."

Both of her friends were fidgeting as Tasha breathed, "I'll take care of you, too, baby. Okay, what happened next?"

"Next, we spent the rest of dinner feeding each other, savoring the food, the spices, and most of all, the sensual act of feeding each other. We didn't speak a word the whole time. It was like the whole evening was focused on the food, our hands, our mouths, and our eyes. It was the sexiest date of my entire life."

"And you said nothing?"

"Not until I dropped him off."

"Did you have to take care of business when you got home?"

"I lost count of how many times. I'm so glad most things are rechargeable these days because I would be out of batteries."

Megan interjected, "It seems like you two had one heck of an evening. Thank you for sharing. How are you feeling now?"

"Confused? Guilty? Aroused? A lot of things, really. Our deal is no sex, no feelings, no strings, and then we basically had food sex."

"Do you have feelings?"

"No! I mean…I don't know. Probably not. I'm not sure."

"Do you want to talk about it?"

"No. I need to think."

Megan snorted. "In my opinion, you need to do less thinking and more feeling." She blushed. "Um, I don't mean to be rude, but I think we need to cut the evening short. You know, because Tasha and I—"

"Yep, I got it. Obviously, I'm gonna go home and do the same...with myself."

It took a while for Mandana to fall asleep, but she felt well-rested when she woke up the next day. Her phone was already brimming with messages from her lawyer, realtor, and various contractors. The first message she opened was the one from Quincy.

Why do I feel relieved to hear from him? It's only been a day and a half...oh, right. We haven't spoken since I dropped him off after dinner. I know how much the evening wound me up. What did it do to him? He wants to meet for coffee this morning to talk. Meeting to talk seems like the harbinger of doom. Why do I care, though? This is strictly platonic. Admittedly, Monday night was a bit wild, but it was an exception. It was also exceptional. Why was the sexiest date of my life a fake date? What does that say about me? I'll tell him I can meet him.

Wow. Today is going to be busy. I need more art for the shop, and I still need a logo. I really need to talk with my parents. Maybe starting my own business will finally get them off my back. Quincy texted back. After he drops Ruby off would be a good time. Hmmm, maybe I could meet him at the school and go from there. Let's see what he says.

Staffing. I need to work on staffing. All right, my top priorities for today are getting some headhunters to find me at least one manager and talking to my parents to tell them about the shop and see if they know any artists. Plus, I have a ton of other stuff to do. Quincy is good with meeting up at the school. Let me see if I can catch Tasha on her walk to school with Sophia. I need to get ready. It's going to be a busy day.

Mandana rolled out of bed and got going. She was fully awake and ready for the day by the time she arrived at Tasha's building. It was less than a minute before Sophia and Tasha walked out, holding hands. "Hey, girl. Ready for your date with Quincy?"

"Good morning to you, too. And it's not a date. He wants to talk."

Tasha's demeanor was suddenly serious. "Uh oh, meeting to talk sounds ominous. Any idea what he wants to talk about?"

"Probably our date on Monday night."

"I figured." Tasha hip bumped her. "Are you okay?"

"I'm a bit worried, but otherwise, all right. Busy day, though. How are you?"

"I'm feeling terrific this morning, and Quincy is taking the munchkins to practice today, so Megan and I will have some *alone time* later."

"Mama Tasha, why did your voice change suddenly?"

"Just something caught in my throat, angel."

Mandana hid a smile behind her hand. "Tasha, I've been meaning to ask you something. Don't answer if you don't want to. I wonder how you are feeling about becoming a second mom to Sophia?"

Tasha's face broke into a sly grin. "There have been challenges and bumps along the road for sure. It's like the entire focus of my life has shifted. Before, I was focused on myself. Now, it's all about this little one. Honestly, though, I have never been happier. Actually, it was a morning like this when I knew my life would never be the same."

"How so?"

"I was about to walk Sophia to school, and she took my hand and said, 'I love you, Aunt Tasha.' And she smiled at me. Five words completely upended my entire life. Do you remember saying that, angel?"

"Yes, Mama Tasha. I still love you."

"I love you, too, munchkin. I know one day you will be big and grown up, and you won't want me to walk you to school anymore, so I am going to treasure every day I can do this with you."

"I will always want you to walk me to school."

"Aw, you're very sweet, munchkin."

Observing the two of them together is amazing. Tasha really seems to love her like she's her own daughter.

"Now, did you ask for any particular reason?"

"Tasha, don't go there. I'm just curious."

"Uh-huh. Just curious. What about you, Sophia? Do you think Miss Mandana would be a good mom?"

"Yes! Miss Mandana is very nice."

"See, Mandana. You'd be a good mom. Sophia means wisdom, so you know what she says is true."

"You're killing me, Tasha."

More evidence proving I can't get more attached. No, not "more attached." I can't get attached at all. That's what I meant. Why did I agree to do this in the first place? I must have been out of my mind.

They saw Quincy and Ruby as they rounded the corner, and they all waved to each other. The girls gave their respective parents a hug and then skipped toward the school, holding hands and giggling.

"Well, all right then. I'll, uh, leave you two to it. Quincy, I'll send you some work later this morning, along with your share from the app and website job for the clothing boutique in Connecticut. Mandana...think about what we talked about. It's the best thing that ever happened to me."

"Later, Tasha." They watched her walk away before Quincy shifted to face Mandana. "What was Tasha talking about?"

"It's nothing."

"The best thing that ever happened to her is nothing?"

I might need to strangle her later.

Something made Quincy decide to back off quickly and raise his hands in surrender. "Okay, okay. Forget I said anything."

Oops.

Mandana smoothed her expression to something she hoped was neutral. "Where would you like to go? The coffee place near where Tasha lives?"

"Sounds great. How are you?"

"Good. I have a busy day ahead of me. How about you?"

"I got another job. Work from home, benefits, thirty-hour work week with overtime beyond thirty, and a fifteen percent pay increase. I could have gotten more money elsewhere, but the guaranteed work-from-home and thirty-hour week was too good to pass up. I get more time with Ruby, more money, and I can do freelance work on days when Megan and Tasha are watching her."

"What did your current job say?"

Quincy snickered. "They are completely screwed, and they just suddenly realized it. I'm the only one holding their systems together.

My last day is Friday. I figure the duct tape will hold for about a week, maybe two if they are lucky, and then there will be a software update, and suddenly everything will fall apart."

"What happens then?"

"Who knows? Maybe they can hire another duct taper in time, but I doubt it. Plus, a new person will take a long time to figure out how I patched everything together. My guess is they will ask me to fix it as a contractor."

"Will you?"

Quincy grinned. "Maybe. My plan is to trot out a stupidly high asking price."

"How stupid?"

"I was thinking ten thousand dollars."

"Per month?"

"Per hour."

They both laughed at corporate buffoonery. "Quincy, you are wicked. I like it a lot. Honestly, ask for twenty and take anything above ten."

Quincy's eyebrows rose. "You think they'll actually pay me?"

"Probably not immediately, no. First, they are going to find someone else who is much less expensive. When the new person fails for the reasons you outlined, then they'll come back to you. Then you ask for twenty-five."

"You are wonderfully cutthroat."

"I have three older brothers, all of whom followed my parent's wishes and went into business. Unfortunately for my brothers, I got all the brains."

"The looks, too." Quincy's face looked suddenly panicked. "Oh, sorry."

I feel like I'm required to glare at him, but I appreciate the compliment.

"So, did your brothers all fail?"

"Nah. Well, Cyrus, the eldest, failed hard. He went into hedge funds and was certain crypto was the future. He lost everything and had to go live with our parents. Almost lost his wife and kids, too, but Dad called in a favor. Now Cyrus is a Vice President of Midwest Strategic Development, based out of Chicago."

"What the hell does the Vice President of Strategic...whatever... even do?"

"No one knows. I'm pretty sure Cyrus doesn't know. Bullshit jobs."

"Yep, bullshit jobs."

"My other brothers are doing well. Unlike Cyrus, they both managed to avoid going into jobs that required any brains. Don't get me wrong, I love them all dearly, but I'm realistic about their gifts. Anyway, between what I've heard from my parents, my brothers, and bartending, I have a pretty good idea of just how your bosses think."

"Honestly, it's a win for me either way. I've already got a better job, and maybe I'll get stupid money on top."

"There you go. All right, let's order. I'm buying this time."

Quincy looked confused. "Wasn't me paying for all of our dates part of the deal?"

"Is this a date?"

"I guess not."

"There you go," Mandana said with a satisfied smirk.

Brighter than my brothers, for sure.

They waited awkwardly for their drinks, then found a quiet corner to sit down.

"Mandana, I want to apologize for Monday night. It got out of hand, and I feel like it's all my fault."

"You mean, eating food right out of my hand?"

"Yeah? I wasn't thinking, and I overstepped."

"Well, it's not entirely your fault, although we can both agree it was definitely your fault at first. I was distraught. It was partially anger, but another part...I was turned on. I just couldn't...I didn't express my emotions in a mature manner. So, when you wanted me to try something, I wanted to get back at you. You were so kind and nervous, and I literally tried to bite the hand you fed me with. I still feel really bad about trying to bite you. Anyway, you feeding me—"

I shouldn't say anything more. Going on is stupid and ill-advised. I'm just going to stop now.

"—I don't know. It's like a switch flipped in my head, and I lost full control over myself."

And I am still talking.

"Then the rest of dinner, feeding each other in silence..."

He finished her thought. "Was amazing. Honestly, it was the best date of my entire life. And it wasn't even a real date, which sounds awful."

I feel the exact same way.

"Quincy, we didn't break the rules, but I feel like we stretched them too far. We can't bend the rules again. After this, it's just vanilla dates."

Vanilla is for the best, for both of us.

"Of course. I was thinking the exact same thing. Strictly platonic."

"So, you don't have any feelings?"

"Exactly. As I said, it was the best date of my life, but it was all fake. For Ruby's sake, I'm glad you are willing to continue after our disaster."

Disaster? I guess he makes sense. He said his only priority is Ruby. Why does his calling it a "disaster" make me feel so miserable?

"Well, I'm glad we cleared the air on this. Maybe we can go on another fake date a week from today."

"Perfect. This time, would you like to pick a place for us to go?"

"That's a good idea, Quincy. I'll text you once I've decided. I'm going to go now because I have a busy day ahead of me." Mandana turned and left with unseemly haste, skipping the usual polite pleasantries in her rush to leave.

Chapter 13

Hot Hot Hot

Arrow

Bewildered by the abrupt end of the conversation, Quincy watched Mandana leave with a heavy heart.

I'm doing the right thing, for Mandana and for Ruby. I shouldn't have lied to her, though. Maintaining our fake relationship is too important, especially now. Maria said Stacy and her new husband will meet with their lawyer in Portland in ten days. They also want to meet Ruby. I can't mess this up any more than I already have.

The truth is, Monday was the best date of my entire life, and more than anything, I wanted it to be real. Mandana is brilliant, compassionate, and beautiful, but I had no idea just how sensual she could be or how fiery and commanding she could be, even without speaking a word.

My priority has to be Ruby, and if it means lying to Mandana about my feelings, then that's what I'll do. I'm just grateful she hasn't broken the whole thing off. Yet. I have to be careful from here on out. I also need to tell Ruby that she is finally about to meet her mother.

Walking back to his place, he stopped at the grocery store. After experiencing Megan's culinary skills, Quincy was very aware of how his own culinary abilities were lacking. Now Ruby was able to make a better lasagna than he could, and apparently, Tasha taught her how to make homemade mac and cheese. Today, he was going to make chili, and he was looking forward to it. Tasha had kindly sent him some recipes to pick from as well as some guidance about the artistry of chili.

The day went quickly, and at noon, he started working on the chili. It would be a long, slow process with periodic stirring. Quincy was using store-bought spices for this batch, but if it went well, Tasha had also provided the name of the company in New Mexico from which she ordered her spices. Once the first batch of spices was in, he went back to work, setting a timer for when to stir and add the next spice load.

Hours later, Quincy set the chili to simmer and, with a final swirl of the spoon, covered it and grabbed his coat. Waiting for the girls in the wet and cold was lonely, but he timed it well so he didn't wait long. He flagged down Ruby and Sophia from the roiling horde of children, receiving two quick hugs before they began their short trek home. Quincy chatted with the girls about their day as he carefully hung up their rain gear to dry. He felt pleased when they asked him what he was cooking because they thought it smelled good.

The girls read and quietly munched on some healthy snacks while he snuck in a bit of work before he had to take them to roller derby practice. They talked excitedly throughout the ride to practice, brief snippets of conversation reaching his ear from the back seat. The Hangar, home of the Rose City Rollers, was a cavernous space that looked very much like the inside of an airplane hangar. Taking up most of the floor was the oval track, where some skaters were already starting to warm up. Quincy struggled to help the girls with their skates and pads and was very relieved when another parent offered to help.

Ruby and Sophia looked as wobbly as baby giraffes on their skates as a teenage coach led them through some exercises. Quincy asked one of the other parents about the teenager's presence. He learned how the league encouraged a good number of the older, more experienced teens to give back to the derby community by training and coaching the next generation. Some of the Rosebuds had been skating competitively for ten years before they graduated high school. Quincy started to look forward to Ruby officially joining the ranks of the Rose Petals, as the younger juniors were called.

Most of today's training involved learning how to fall safely, a much-needed skill. Quincy winced every time Ruby hit the track, but she wasn't crying, and she got up after every fall, planned or not. Some of the less new skaters engaged in drills and strategy in another area of the track. At the end of practice, the two girls gingerly skated over to the bleachers to take off their skates and gear. Getting them out of their gear was more straightforward than getting them in. Looking around at other skaters, it seemed like it wouldn't be long before the girls would be perfectly capable of handling their gear on their own. Soon, he would just be their chauffeur and cheerleader.

Back in the car, Quincy asked, "What's your roller derby name, Sophia?"

"Wycked Wytch, spelled W-Y-C-K-E-D -W-Y-T-C-H."

"I like it."

"Me too! Wyrm and I are going to be great one day!"

"Oh, you're right. I need to call you by your derby name."

"You see, Wyrm. He picks up on things eventually," Wycked Wytch whispered sotto voce.

"Definitely, Wytch. I wonder how long it will take him to bring Miss Mandana over for dinner?" Wyrm was barely pretending to whisper.

"Maybe we should see if his chili is any good first," Wytch opined.

They definitely know I can hear them. I'm being manipulated by a pair of eight-year-olds. Hang on. What do they mean I will pick up on things eventually?

Dinner was actually really good. Quincy served the chili over rice with shredded cheese and sour cream. He also had a side of roasted broccoli, which the girls liberally sprinkled with more cheese and sour cream, but they did eat the broccoli.

"This is really good, Daddy!"

"Thank you, sweetheart."

His traitorous daughter grinned at him. "*So,*" Ruby drawled. "Is there anyone else you want to cook for?"

"I really like cooking for you two. What should I make for Friday?"

"Daddy, you know what I mean." There was whispering between the two girls, who then stared at him with crossed arms and twin scowls.

I'm being railroaded by eight-year-olds. I'm not sure if I'm terrified or impressed.

"Girls, I don't think Miss Mandana and I are yet at the 'inviting each other over for dinner' point in our relationship. When I feel we are, then I will invite her over for dinner. I promise."

The twin scowls faded to frowns, quickly changing into smiles when he brought out ice cream. Tasha showed up not long after the girls finished their ice cream, looking freshly showered. "Did you have a quiet and relaxing afternoon by yourself?"

"Quincy Rogers, get your mind out of the gutter," Tasha retorted with mock offense.

"I have to. There's not enough room in the gutter for your mind and mine."

Tasha paused and mockingly pondered his statement. "True, very true." She then leaned in close and whispered, "Megan and I had dinner tonight, Mandana and Quincy style."

"Oh, God. She told you?"

"Mandana gave us a very detailed recounting last night." Tasha's voice dropped again. "It was so damn hot. Megan and I found it to be *very* inspirational."

"Um, thanks?"

"Good boy, Quincy. *Good boy.* Oh, how was your chili?"

"Really good. I liked the cinnamon. I'm going to get spices from the place in New Mexico you mentioned. I feel like a blend of different chiles will enhance the flavor, and then I can start to play with the amounts."

"Aw, you're adorable. Can I try it?"

"Sure, let me get you a spoon."

"Is it hot?"

"Definitely."

"Let me see." Tasha scooped up a heaping spoonful and gave it a hearty sniff. She eyed it carefully before putting it in her mouth. She chewed slowly, savoring the chili like a sommelier with a glass of wine. "Not bad. Not bad at all. Medium heat, good flavor blend."

"Medium heat?"

"Yes, or what I like to call, White boy hot. I grew up on Pappa's chili, and it would toast you Black, or at least dark brown." Tasha laughed and patted his cheek. "We'll invite you over the next time Megan makes vindaloo. For a White girl, she knows how to cook spicy food."

"I can see why you are marrying her, then."

"It ain't only for her cookin', sugah." Tasha's native South Carolina accent rose to the surface. "Come on, now, Wycked Wytch. I gotta get you home to yer momma. You say your goodbyes, and I'll git yer coat."

"Bye, Book Wyrm! Bye, Mister Quincy!"

Megan is a lucky woman.

Chapter 14

Foolin'

Def Leppard

The potluck on Sunday wasn't a formal affair, but Megan and Tasha encouraged Mandana to dress nicely as they were hoping the meal would be the sort of nice event they could do again. She examined her white dress with one shoulder uncovered, the blue sash at her waist, and her comfortable wedge-heeled sandals and decided it passed muster.

White is a terrible idea for a potluck. I'm going to spill something. It does look really nice, though, and I never have the chance to wear it. I could wear this for Quincy sometime. Nope. Not going to go there. He made it very clear on Wednesday how our date was a disaster for the plan, and the whole thing is strictly platonic. Plus, he's not going to be here today. Stop thinking about Quincy. You look amazing in this dress. It goes perfectly with your skin tone. You aren't going to spill anything. It's perfect.

When Mandana arrived, the potluck was in full swing. Megan let her in and took her coat before returning to check-in. "What did you bring? It looks amazing."

"Thank you. This is a Persian dish called *ghormeh sabzi*. It's an herb stew with beans, beef, or lamb, in this case, beef, spinach, and limes, served with basmati rice."

"I can't wait to try it. First, can I introduce you to some people?"

"Sure."

"This is Maria and her girlfriend, Savannah. Next, we have Leslie and John, Leslie and I seem always to be subbing at the same schools. And this is Pete and Tim. Pete used to work with Tasha."

Mandana greeted everyone in turn. After being introduced, she quietly asked Megan, "Is this the Maria who apparently knows everyone?"

"She's the one."

"Damn, she is imposing. Her girlfriend is gorgeous."

"Maria has a type, and her type is beautiful. She was the first woman Tasha dated."

"Oh." Realization caught up with Mandana. "*Oh*...and you're cool with...?"

"I'm fine with it. Let's just say Maria has been exceptionally supportive of my relationship with Tasha."

"I hear a story there."

Megan smiled demurely. "Another time."

Just then, Mandana heard a familiar male voice.

Mandana whispered furiously, "Megan...you didn't say *he* was going to be here."

Megan adopted a look of pure innocence. "Oops. Did I forget to mention that we invited Quincy?"

"*You did,*" Mandana growled.

"On the plus side, you look absolutely stunning in your dress." Megan giggled playfully.

They are meddling again. Well, I do look—he's seen me. By his expression, I guess stunning is the right word. Damn, he looks good, too. This is getting too complicated.

"You know, Megan, our entire relationship is fake, right?"

"We know. We're just trying to support you two. You know, we're helping to build the plausible story of your whirlwind romance." Megan's attempted look of pure innocence was back.

I'll give her credit; she is really trying her best to look and sound innocent. I don't believe her for a second. Would it really be so bad if they got their way? Maybe? I don't want kids. Then again, Tasha didn't, and she is incredibly happy being Sophia's other mom. Maybe it's time to get to know Ruby. What the hell am I thinking? Strictly platonic and no danger to Ruby. We have a deal.

"—and, of course, you already know Mandana," Tasha said as she completed the introductions. Tasha went back to speak with another guest, but Megan somehow slipped away, leaving Mandana and Quincy standing together.

"Hi."

"Hi."

"Did they tell you I was going to be here?"

Quincy shook his head. "Nope. You?"

Mandana sighed heavily. "Nope."

In the awkward manner of someone deliberately changing the subject, Quincy asked, "What did you bring?"

"*Ghormeh sabzi*. It's a Persian stew served on rice. What about you?" Mandana said proudly.

"Nothing nearly as awesome. I made chicken parmesan."

"Are you Italian?"

Quincy chuckled. "Not at all, but the English aren't known for their cooking, and it looked like something I could make."

"You're smart to go with what you're good at."

He gave her a quizzical look. "You never say Iran or Iranian, do you?"

"I don't. It's a personal thing. The land was Persia long before it was Iran. It was Persia before the Prophet's people left Mecca. It was Persia before Alexander came along. It will always be Persia to me."

"Have you been there?"

She shook her head ruefully. "My parents and grandparents fled when the Shah fell, and the ayatollahs aren't exactly friendly to people of our faith."

"But you're an atheist."

Mandana responded with a hint of sarcasm. "Also, not popular in a theocracy."

"True."

She shrugged. "Anyway, I have no interest in getting scooped up as a spy and held for years in the ayatollah's prisons, getting assaulted on a daily basis while I wait to be traded for a billion dollars in humanitarian aid."

"When you put it that way, I can see why you haven't gone there."

The silence that followed quickly got awkward.

After some fidgeting, Quincy said nervously, "Hey, I need a favor."

"What kind of favor?"

"Stacy and her husband are coming to town, and she wants to meet Ruby. Maria advised me it is best to be accommodating at this stage in case we go to trial. Would you be there with me? You know, as my fake girlfriend?"

"What time?"

"Saturday, at noon. We're meeting at Powell's downtown."

"Public place, multiple exits, always crowded. Not a bad choice."

"Thanks...I wasn't even thinking on a security level."

Mandana could hear the edge in her response. "You're a man; you don't generally have to."

"Oh..."

She grinned wickedly. "All right, it's time for a bit of payback."

"What?" Poor Quincy looked utterly lost.

"Let's get some food because I'm hungry. Also, I need to talk to our meddling friends."

"I'm hungry, too."

As she ate, Mandana's mind drifted along her stream of consciousness. *I have no idea what kind of person this Stacy is, but we are definitely bringing backup. Quincy needs a couple of tasteful tattoos. He would look even hotter and it would drive my mother crazy. Why am I thinking about introducing him to my mother right now? Oh, his chicken parm is pretty good.*

Mandana stalked closer to her friend like a lion in tall grass. Once close, she hissed, "Hello, Tasha. So kind of you and Megan to invite both me and Quincy and conveniently forget to tell either of us."

"Oops. It must have slipped our minds."

"Uh-huh.

Tasha was unable to maintain her attempt at innocence. She folded guiltily. "All right, I'm sorry."

"It's fine; however, penance is required."

"How so?" Tasha asked hopefully.

"Quincy, Ruby, and I are all meeting Quincy's ex and her new husband at Powell's on Saturday."

"Oh, good location."

"Yeah, I know. I want you three there as a backup in case this Stacy bitch pulls something. I hope not, but it would be handy to have witnesses there. If things get weird for Ruby, having Sophia nearby as a friend could help."

"Absolutely. We will be there for the three of you." Tasha laid a hand on Mandana's arm. "Hey, thank you for looking out for

Quincy and Ruby. I am really sorry about not telling you Quincy would be here. It wasn't fair to either of you."

"Thanks, Tasha."

"Oh, girl, I'm not done." Tasha held her head up proudly. "I might be sorry, but I would still do it again. Do you want to know why?"

"Yes, why?"

"Because you are standing here, asking for help to save Quincy and Ruby. You care, Mandana. You care about people, but specifically, you care about *them*." Tasha held up her hand before Mandana could speak. "I know what you are going to say. You'll tell me some bullshit about how it is platonic, no strings, just helping someone out, but I think we both know none of it is true anymore."

Shit, shit, shit, shit, shit. *She's right. The amount of effort I have made to keep trying to convince myself to stick to the deal is evidence enough I don't really want to.*

The realization must have been plain on Mandana's face because Tasha placed a friendly hand on Mandana's arm. "Trust me, I know exactly how terrifying your realization is. It was Megan's husband, Brad, who saw I was in love with her. It shocked the hell out of me."

"What happened?"

"I told Megan I loved her, and then she told me the same."

"Everything was good, then, right?"

Tasha shook her head. "Yes and no. Afterward, we both figured saying 'I love you' was enough, and we stopped communicating. Things got bad, fast. Then we started talking honestly again, and things got better. I know you think I'm horny all the time, and that's generally true, but it's also part of how Megan and I communicate. We try to be open and non-judgmental."

"I understand you more now and kinda admire it."

"Also, just look at her." She gazed at her partner, and Mandana saw genuine love and care on Tasha's face. "She's my everything. Well, her and Sophia...anyway, back to you. What are you going to do?"

"What can I do? Quincy made it clear our last date was a disaster, and we have to stick to the deal."

Tasha grunted derisively in response.

"Would you talk—"

"Sweetie, this isn't high school. I'm not going to pass Quincy notes in class."

Mandana's shoulders slumped in defeat. "Oh, sorry."

"It's okay. I'm happy to talk with you anytime you want, but you're a big girl and you'll eventually have to talk with Quincy. When you do, be honest. I mean, *completely* honest."

"Thanks, Tasha."

"Come here and give me a hug."

Tasha's embrace felt warm and comforting.

"Thank you again. Has anyone ever told you that you give good hugs?"

"Yes, actually. Oh, and one more piece of advice: Let Ruby get to know you. If you are going to be serious about Quincy, then you have to be serious about Ruby, too."

"I know. Honestly, Ruby is such an amazing kid. I like her a lot and want her to like me."

"Good, now go mingle. I need to tell my fiancée how much I love her."

Tasha is right about everything. Also, Megan is a lucky woman.

Mandana walked over to where Ruby and Sophia were sitting and gently folded herself down onto the floor to join them. She nodded at their plates and said, "Hi, you two. Did you like the food?"

Sophia answered, "Yes, it was very good, Miss Mandana!"

"What about you, Ruby? Did you try the *ghoram sabzi*?"

"I did. It was delicious, Miss Mandana! I even had seconds."

Mandana smiled genuinely. "Really? That's quite the compliment. Would you like to try more Persian food?"

"Yes, I would."

"I'll talk to your dad. And I see Nocturne and Julius are enjoying the party, too." The two cats were curled up and napping between the girls. Nocturne popped open an eye when her name was mentioned, then went back to sleep. "How is your book club going?"

"It's just us right now, but that's okay. We hope some of the other skaters might join."

"Right, the roller derby. Megan was telling me about that. Is it fun?"

"So far. Wytch and I are still on basic skills right now. We hope to get on a home team by September."

"Witch?"

"Sophia's derby name is Wycked Wytch, spelled with y's, and my name is Book Wyrm, also spelled with y. We picked our own names," Ruby announced proudly.

Mandana smiled at her. "You two are awesome. I love your names, and I want to come see you two skate."

Ruby gave her a curious look. "Miss Mandana? Are you and Daddy boyfriend and girlfriend?"

She asks tough questions.

"Um."

"Have you kissed him?" After Ruby asked this, the two girls collapsed into a giggling fit.

You are killing me, kid. Those poor cats look so confused.

"No, we haven't kissed."

Yet, I hope.

"Why not? Daddy likes you," Ruby stated guilelessly.

Sophia chimed in, "I used to think kissing was yucky, but now I think it is nice. Mommy really likes kissing Mama Tasha."

"Your Daddy likes me, huh?" Mandana struggled to hide a happy grin.

Ruby nodded. "He doesn't say it, but I can tell," she asserted. "You are very pretty and smart. He smiles when he thinks about you."

Sophia added, "Daddy never made Mommy smile like Mama Tasha does. Her smile is how I knew Mommy and Mama Tasha loved each other."

"You girls are very wise." Mandana nodded sagely.

And far too observant sometimes. I like knowing he smiles when he thinks about me.

Ruby giggled. "See! That's what I'm talking about."

Mandana was confused. "What?"

"You just smiled like Daddy does, Miss Mandana. Were you thinking about my Daddy?"

Damn, this girl is sharp.

"Um, I think I need to go and get more food. You girls have fun."

She rose with unseemly haste, leaving the two girls whispering and giggling behind her.

Chapter 15

Shake Me

Cinderella

Wednesday night found Quincy searching for parking in Chinatown.

This is a terrible idea. Why the hell did I agree to this? Oh, right, because my eight-year-old is manipulating me again. Did she plan this with Mandana, or did she come up with this all on her own? I can't believe Ruby would come up with something like this on her own. Actually, maybe I can. Maybe Sophia helped. I might be getting paranoid.

Quincy thought back to the end of the potluck on Sunday. He had been standing and talking with Mandana, Megan, and Tasha before he was interrupted.

A little tug at his sleeve, and there was Ruby, standing beside him, looking perfectly innocent. Then she says she really liked Mandana's Persian food and wanted more. Of course, there weren't any leftovers, so Mandana says instead of going on a date tonight, Ruby and I should come over for a home-cooked Persian dinner. Suddenly, everyone is looking at me. What was I supposed to say? No? Obviously not. So, of course, I have to say yes. My number one goal is to make sure Ruby doesn't get attached, and now I'm completely blowing it.

He found parking and texted Mandana. Bundling Ruby out into the wet Portland night, they raced over to Mandana's building. She buzzed them in, and they shook the water off in the foyer. Her apartment door opened after one knock. Quincy looked up from Ruby, who had taken hold of his hand. He took a look at the woman standing in the open doorway and forgot how to breathe. Mandana wore a long dress, a deep scarlet in color, and elaborate beadwork across the chest and arms. Around her waist, she wore a broad gold embroidered belt. Her hair was pulled into a high ponytail, framed by delicate gold netting.

"Hi, Ruby. It's good to see you again."

"Hi, Miss Mandana," Ruby responded cheerfully.

"Miss Tasha has been teaching you such good manners. Unlike your father, who is standing there catching flies."

Ruby giggled. "You look like a princess."

"Thank you, Ruby. In Persia, if I were the daughter of a king, then I would be a *shahdokht*. Can you say that?"

"*Shahdokht!*"

"Very good, Ruby." Mandana's smile was as captivating as her dress.

"Hi, Mandana."

She grinned at him, delight and mischief dancing in her eyes. "Well, hello, Quincy."

"You look—"

"Stunning." Mandana chuckled at Quincy's obvious discomfort. "Come on in. Let me get your coats. Feel free to look around."

Nice place. A bit minimalist, but the decorations look expensive...

"Mandana, are these real?" Quincy pointed at two frames on the wall.

"The jerseys? Yes, they are real. Signed, not printed, from the 2014 finals in Miami. They aren't game-worn or anything, though."

"How many Hall of Fame players signed these?"

"Six, I think. Plus, some like LeBron who aren't in the Hall yet."

Holy shit, those two jerseys must be worth a fortune. No wonder she keeps them behind glass. Wow.

"I assume the rugs are all Persian."

"You assume correctly. And before you ask, this dress is as well."

"Your dress matches my name!"

"It does, Ruby." Mandana bent down to look his daughter in the eye. "Would you like to come and help me in the kitchen? I hear you are becoming quite the cook."

"Who told you?"

"Miss Megan and Miss Tasha did. Can you stir this stew for me while I get drinks for everyone? Also, what would you like to drink?"

"Do you have soda?"

"I do, but only if your dad says soda is okay."

Quincy nodded his approval. "She can have a little bit of soda and also a glass of water. I would like water as well. Tap is fine. We don't need the fancy stuff."

"Good, I prefer tap. At least in Portland, it's clean and inexpensive."

"Speaking of expensive, your decorations are very tasteful and classy."

"Thank you. I've moved a lot, so I prefer to have a few high-quality items rather than a bunch of random stuff. I do have a weakness for books, though." Mandana slid some glasses over the counter and then turned back to Ruby. "You are doing a great job. How is the texture? Is it thin like a soup or thick like a stew?"

"It feels thick to me."

"Perfect. You can stop stirring because we are about to eat."

I don't see another room. Where are we eating?

"Um, Mandana. I'm sorry if I sound stupid, but where is your table?"

"We are eating Persian food, and we are eating it Persian style." Quincy watched Mandana shake a cloth out and place it on a soft rug in the center of the main room. "This cloth is called a *sufra*, and this is how Persians have eaten for centuries. There is no head of the table and no foot. We are all equal. I can provide stools or pillows if you need them."

"Out of curiosity, is this how you ate growing up?"

"Yes and no. My parents have a table like most Americans, and we use it a lot. But we always used the *sufra* for holidays and special occasions."

Fascinating. She's like an onion with endless layers. Modern, sophisticated, and liberated, yet at the same time, she has an ironclad connection to her cultural past.

Quincy buried his skepticism, although he did worry about his back. "I'm looking forward to trying this, although I may take you up on those cushions really soon."

I would ask Ruby how she is doing with eating on the floor, but clearly, she is fine.

"Miss Mandana, Sophia, and I ate like this at the potluck. I like eating Persian style."

Mandana smiled adoringly at Ruby. "You did. Well, let's see how your father fares. I am going to start us off tonight with *adasi*, a lentil soup."

"What's a lentil?" Ruby asked.

"A lentil is a vegetable, a type of legume. Other types of legumes are beans or chickpeas. They taste good, and they are high in protein."

"Cool."

Mandana looked at him. "Do you two say prayers or anything before eating?"

"Not really, no."

"All right, then, please, enjoy."

They all tucked in with gusto. After everyone had a few mouthfuls, Mandana asked, "What do you think?"

"It's so good!"

"Thank you. What about you, Quincy?"

"I like it a lot. It reminds me of split pea soup but with more spices and a chunkier texture. Are there potatoes in here?"

"Yes, there are. A relatively new addition to an ancient dish. Good catch."

Eating this way is awkward, but the food is so good that I don't care.

Once everyone had finished the soup, Mandana cleared their dishes and called for Ruby to join her in the kitchen.

"Can I help?"

"No, you just relax. We're going to have some girl talk while I get the next course ready."

I should probably be worried.

"Ruby, did you have practice today? I'm sorry, I forgot. Your name is Book Wyrm."

Quincy could hear the glee in Ruby's voice as she answered, "It was so good! Wytch and I are getting better every time."

"Do you know when you will skate in a game?"

"No. Not for a long time. We still have a lot to learn. I hope we can be on home teams in the fall."

"Will you play together?"

"We really want to. We want to be on the Skaters of Doom."

"That's a fun team name. What are the others?"

"Killer Bees and Bad Apples."

Mandana's laughter was like a fast-running stream, energetic and musical. "I love the team names and your derby names. It's great you are having fun and getting better."

"When will you come to watch me skate?"

Oh, no.

"I would love to, but I think I'll need to ask your dad first."

"Oh, it's okay. Daddy will say yes if I ask him."

I will? Actually, I probably will. I'm such a sucker. This is the attachment I was worried about.

"Can you take this out? This is *baghali polo*, a flavorful rice dish."

"Okay!"

"And I'll bring out the *khoresht fesenjen*. This is a walnut and pomegranate stew with lamb."

The scents teased Quincy's nostrils. "Mandana, this smells incredible."

"Thank you. I hope you enjoy the meal. Oh! I forgot the spinach. Be right back." Mandana returned quickly. "The spinach has a bit of spice. Does anyone need more to drink? Quincy, when you have the chance, I would love to hear how your new job is going."

"Sure. Once I try everything, of course. Oh, wow. This is really good. What do you think, sweetheart?"

"I like it so much. Thank you, Miss Mandana!"

"To answer your earlier question, the new job is going well. I'm still learning their software and figuring out their duct tape, but nothing unexpected. I have more flexibility in my hours, which I love."

"Right, the lower hours and greater flexibility are awesome. I keep hearing about some companies experimenting with reduced hours for the same pay."

"Yes, this is one of them. Greater productivity, better employee morale, and higher retention rates. It's working really well for them."

"And working well for you, too. I would ask why more companies don't do this, but I feel like we both know the answer to this."

"Yep, *Bullshit Jobs*. Sorry, Ruby. Daddy said a bad word."

"It's okay, Daddy. I learned most of the bad words in first grade."

Quincy gave Mandana a dirty look as she collapsed in laughter. "Somehow, I don't feel better. Mandana, feel free to stop laughing at any time." She laughed even harder.

Defeated, Quincy went back to the food. Eating his feelings seemed like the best plan. The rest of the dinner went well. Mandana provided an update about her cat cafe, a concept that Ruby absolutely adored. The two of them talked about the cafe for a while.

I really like how Mandana speaks with Ruby. She isn't dumbing things down, and she appears to be taking Ruby's questions and ideas seriously. It would be so easy to be condescending or dismissive, but Mandana isn't doing any of that. I'm impressed.

"I'm sorry to break this up, but I need to get Ruby home and in bed. She has school in the morning."

"*Dad.* You're no fun."

"I know, sweetheart. It's part of the job sometimes."

"Thank you for dinner, Miss Mandana. It was very good, and I liked eating Persian style. I want to eat like that at home."

"Yes, thank you so much for dinner. It was wonderful. Can I help clean up before we go?"

"No, I've got it. It was my pleasure to cook for you both."

"Aren't you going to kiss Miss Mandana good night?"

What? It's another trap. Damn, Ruby is way too bright.

"Um, sure." Quincy shrugged apologetically and gave Mandana a brief kiss on the cheek.

"Dad! Don't you know how to kiss? On the lips, silly."

Please no.

Mandana shrugged at him in a manner that suggested she was okay with it. They both leaned in for an instantaneous peck on the lips.

Ruby pouted at them. "No, I meant a real kiss, like boyfriend and girlfriend."

I'm getting manipulated by an eight-year-old. Again. Uh oh, here she comes.

Mandana leaned in slowly, her scarlet dress shimmering and the gold netting in her hair sparkling. She stopped, her lips hovering just beyond his. He could smell the intoxicating blend of her hair, her perfume, and the spices from her cooking. Quincy shut his eyes and closed the tiny gap. Their lips met, and his mind exploded.

The kiss started softly but firmly. As their lips lingered, Mandana and Quincy's arms moved and met, snaking around each other's torsos. The first touch of fingers lingering on spines sent electricity to their mouths. Quincy could feel Mandana's jaw working as her lips frantically undulated against his. Like a dragon emerging from its lair, her tongue brushed his teeth, and suddenly, their tongues wrestled like Hercules and Antaeus. Then, as quickly as the frenzy had come upon them, the wave broke, and they parted, panting for air.

What the hell?

"Come on, Daddy. Time to go. Bye, Miss Mandana." Ruby sounded perfectly satisfied.

As he stumbled down the hallway after his daughter, Quincy could vaguely make out Ruby saying, "I'm glad you gave Miss Mandana a proper kiss. It's really sad it took you three tries."

Kids...

<u>Chapter 16</u>

Tell It To My Heart

Taylor Dayne

Taylor Dayne

Standing in stunned silence, Mandana watched the door close. In a daze, she barred the door behind them and gathered the dinner dishes and leftovers. As her mind reeled from their kiss, Mandana picked up the phone and called Megan.

"Hi, Mandana. What's up? Hello?"

She shook her head to clear the kiss-induced fog from her mind. "Oh, sorry. Hi, Megan."

"How was your date?"

"Um, I'm not sure what just happened."

"Good or bad?"

"Good, I think. Maybe *really* good."

"Hang on a sec. Tasha, can you finish getting Sophia in bed? I need to talk to Mandana." Mandana waited, listening to one-half of Megan's conversation with her family. "Good, she thinks. Yeah, I'll find out. Thanks, beautiful. Good night, angel. Okay, sorry. Where were we?"

"Ah, my date."

"You sound a bit out of it right now. What happened?"

"We kissed."

"Really? Hang on." Mandana heard gleeful giggling and dancing. "Sorry, I'm back. Tell me more."

"I'm not sure where to start."

"With the kiss? At the beginning? Your choice."

"I spent the afternoon fixing authentic Persian food."

"You're a fantastic cook, I know. What are you wearing?"

"A long, deep scarlet dress with elaborate beadwork."

"Uh-huh. What else?" Megan asked enthusiastically.

"Um, a gold belt, and I have a gold net in my hair."

"Sounds beautiful, tell me more."

"My hair is done up in a high ponytail."

"Awesome, now what was Quincy wearing?"

"He had on jeans and Doc Martens. And a really tight T-shirt under a blazer. It did good things for his chest."

"Uh-huh."

"Do you want to know what Ruby was wearing?"

"Nope, just you and Quincy. What happened? Actually, let's just skip to the kiss."

"The kiss. Ruby wanted us to kiss, so he gave me this little peck on the cheek."

Megan grumped. "Ugh, you're killing me."

"What?"

"Never mind, what happened next?"

"Ruby told him it wasn't a proper kiss and to kiss me on the lips."

Megan perked up. "Oh, how was it?"

"Nothing really, just a quick peck."

"Really?"

"Yes..."

"Come on, Mandana. You can't be calling me because of a 'nothing' kiss."

Mandana took a deep breath and exhaled. "Then Ruby told him it wasn't a real kiss, and he needed to kiss me properly."

"Were you okay with him kissing you?"

"Yes. Excited, actually. I leaned in, but not all the way."

"Mmm hmm, what then?"

"He kissed me for real. It was good, but not great. But then we got closer, and before I knew it, our arms were around each other. Suddenly, it was a real kiss. Like, a real passionate kiss where our lips were just going at it."

There was unexpected silence on the other end of the line.

"Megan, are you still there?"

"Sorry. Your story got me a bit distracted."

"Oh my God. Were you thinking of kissing Tasha?"

Megan sounded embarrassed. "Okay, yes. Look, in my defense, you and Quincy are both really hot, and Tasha is being all maternal right now, and it's all getting me worked up."

"Ugh, fine. Horndog. Where was I?"

"Lips going at it."

"Got it. And then I put a bit of tongue in his mouth, and we were off to the races."

"*Oh, Goddess.*"

"We tongue wrestled for a while, and then we stopped. Ruby reminded Quincy she had school in the morning and they left."

"What? They just left?" Megan exclaimed in shock.

"Um, yeah."

Megan laughed uproariously. "Wow, Mandana. You got played by an eight-year-old. Quincy, too."

"What do you mean?"

"She parent-trapped you. Well, not the full parent trap, but close enough."

"What does 'parent-trapped' mean?"

"Ruby wanted to get you two together, and she engineered a way to do it."

Mandana scoffed. "That's impossible. No eight-year-old could be so devious."

Why is Megan laughing so hard? Could an eight-year-old actually be that cunning?

"Oh, you poor, innocent girl. I have an eight-year-old, and trust me; they can be incredibly crafty sometimes. Actually, the more I think about it, Sophia and Ruby have been whispering a lot lately. Yeah, you got snookered."

Mandana's head was spinning. "Wow. I'm unsure how I feel about being outmaneuvered by an eight-year-old."

"Let's skip that for now. How do you feel about kissing Quincy?"

"Megan, it was amazing. I've been on the edge of breaking the rules, and this may have pushed me over," Mandana gushed.

"Tasha told me about your talk. I'm very excited for you. For both of you."

"I'm excited but nervous. I just wish I knew where Quincy's mind was on this. He keeps saying he wants to protect Ruby from getting attached, but if she's manipulating us like this, then clearly, that ship has sailed. I just hope the ship in question isn't the Titanic."

"For what it's worth, I don't think you and Quincy are on the Titanic, although if you are, I am sure you would share a giant door with him."

"Oh, definitely."

"Good. You two have great chemistry. How is your relationship with Ruby?"

"Oh, Megan," Mandana sighed happily. "Ruby and I had a really nice talk tonight. She's really smart...which I now see can be used in devious ways. I'm starting to see what Tasha was saying."

"And what did Tasha say?" Megan asked with palpable interest.

"She told me how she didn't really ever imagine having a kid and how now she couldn't imagine life without Sophia. Oh, and how you and Sophia are the best and most important parts of her life."

"She's told me the same thing, but it just sounds different hearing it through someone else."

"Are you crying?"

"Yes. I love Tasha so much."

"Now I'm crying, too. The two of you really are perfect together. The three of you, really."

"Maybe you can find love, too. If you want it."

I think I want it. Quincy is a good man, and Ruby is a handful, but in a good way. But does he want me in the same way? Was he truthful about not wanting more kids? If he wasn't, then we have a problem—a big *problem.*

Megan interrupted Mandana's reverie. "Hey, Tasha is done putting Sophia to bed, and I really need to express just how much I love her."

"Thanks for talking. Go and love your future wife."

"Good night, Mandana. Call us if you need anything."

"Good night." She hung up and turned back to the dishes.

What am I going to do now? Clearly, the fake thing is no longer working for me, and if Quincy's kiss tonight tells me anything, then it's not working for him, either. We really need to talk about what happened tonight, but I don't think right now is a good time. I have to hand it to wily little Ruby; she sure knows how to shake things up.

Chapter 17
The Policy of Truth
Depeche Mode

Quincy had mainly recovered by the time they got home. He couldn't help but notice how very proud of herself Ruby seemed. As he tucked her into bed, Quincy asked, "I know we usually read before you go to bed, but maybe tonight we can talk instead?"

"Okay. What would you like to talk about?"

"A few things, actually."

I feel like such an asshole for not telling her this sooner. It's like if I don't tell her, then it won't be true. Unfortunately, it is true, and she deserves to know.

"I heard from your mom."

Ruby looked at him excitedly. "Really?"

"Yes. She and her new husband are coming to Portland this weekend. She wants to meet you."

"She's married now?"

"Yes. I don't know when she got married, but it seems like she is. There's something else. She wants you to live with her. In Florida."

Ruby frowned. "But we live here."

"Yes, we do live here. This is your home, and it always will be. She does want to meet you soon. How do you feel about that?"

"Do I have to live with her?" She asked plaintively.

"She wants to try and gain custody. Do you know what custody means?"

"*Dad.* I'm eight, but I read a lot. It's like a divorce, except you and mom were never married."

"You really are a smart kid. I have a lawyer, and we are going to figure this all out together. Do you remember Miss Maria from the party?"

Now, I'm referring to adults like Tasha does. Actually, that's probably not a bad thing. Ruby has needed a mom for her whole life, and now, with this whole switching afternoon watching the girls thing, she at least gets some good influences from Megan and Tasha.

"Yes, she looked fierce. Her girlfriend was very pretty."

"Miss Maria *is* fierce." Quincy paused, not sure how to continue. "How do you feel about meeting your mom?"

"I'm excited, Daddy, but also a bit scared. I mean, maybe Mom is really nice, but I've never met her, so I don't really know." Ruby looked thoughtful. "It would be better if she lived here. Then I could see both of you."

"I agree. I could move to Florida if you want."

"Not really. I like it here. Plus, Sophia is here, and she's my best friend."

"You only met her a few weeks ago."

"*Dad.*" Ruby's tone strongly implied that Quincy was as dumb as a bag of hammers. "Sophia is like a sister to me. Plus, we are going to grow up to be roller derby stars together."

Why do I always feel like my daughter is much more intelligent and wiser than me? I know I'm not stupid, but she somehow runs circles around me. Maybe she will manage not to do all of the dumb shit I did. One thing is for sure: I couldn't be more proud of her.

"One thing you learn as you get older is your family isn't just the people you are related to by blood. Family is also the people you choose to surround yourself with. I'm glad you consider Sophia to be your sister."

"What about Miss Mandana? Do you want her to be part of our family?"

How does she manage to look so innocent when I suspect there is some multi-layered plot going on inside her head? Maybe she is as innocent as she appears. No, no, she's not. The way she manipulated our kiss tonight. Dammit, I hate being constantly outsmarted by an eight-year-old.

Quincy turned the question back to Ruby. "Do you?"

"I asked first," Ruby pointed out triumphantly.

Dammit. I should have seen that coming. All right. What is my answer? Clearly, this whole deal we have isn't working for me. Or Ruby, for that matter. Somehow, I have to make this real.

"I really like Miss Mandana, and I think I would like her to be part of our family. Unfortunately, I don't know if she wants the same thing."

"I dunno, Dad. The way she kissed you..." Ruby covered her face and started giggling wildly.

"You tricked us..."

The giggling mercifully stopped. "*Dad.* I'm only eight. How could I have tricked you?" Ruby immediately started giggling again.

Nothing prepares you for the moment when you realize your child —The child you have loved and cared for since birth—is capable of such boundless devilry. She's mocking me to my face, and I can't even be angry about it. I need to find a book for stupid parents raising a genius child. Maybe there are support groups. I hope there are support groups.

"You are obviously innocent, my beloved little genius. I've answered your question, now you can answer mine. Do you want Miss Mandana to be part of our family?"

"Of course, Dad. She's very smart, and I like how she talks with me. Most adults just want to talk about school, and then they don't know what else to talk with me about. Miss Mandana isn't like other grown-ups. When we talked about her cat cafe, she listened to my ideas, and even if she didn't like them, she didn't treat me like a dumb kid. I think she liked my idea about a kids and kittens playroom."

"You had a really good idea."

"Thanks, Daddy! Also, Miss Mandana is an excellent cook."

"I'm not?" Quincy wasn't sure how to take this.

"You try really hard, and I love you."

Dagger through the heart. A very subtle yet brutal dagger. If I'm being honest, she's not wrong. The truth still hurts, though.

"I've been talking with Miss Megan and Miss Tasha about how to be better in the kitchen. I have some more time and money now, so I'm going to take some cooking classes."

"You're the best Dad ever."

"So, you wouldn't mind if things got serious between me and Miss Mandana?"

Wow. Her look speaks volumes. Encyclopedia Britannica-level of volumes.

"She makes you smile, Daddy. I want you to be happy. Plus, I approve of her, so don't mess this up," Ruby admonished him.

"I'll try my best."

"Yoda says, 'Do or do not, there is no try.' I'm sleepy. Good night, Daddy."

"Good night, sweetheart."

She quoted Yoda to me. I didn't think I could be prouder of her, but I am.

Quincy turned off the light but left Ruby's door open. Sure enough, Dolly Purrton glided past his legs, making her way onto Ruby's bed to cuddle with her favorite human. He watched from the doorway as Dolly made biscuits in the blanket, purring loud enough that he could hear her from across the room, her paws rhythmically working to ensure a soft resting place. Once Dolly curled up, he padded quietly toward his room, turning off the lights behind him.

Picking up his phone, he texted Mandana.

Quincy: *We should probably talk about tonight.*

As he brushed his teeth, his phone buzzed, indicating a response.

Mandana: *Yes, we do. Not tonight. Can we meet tomorrow?*

Quincy: *I'll ask Tasha to watch Ruby.*

Mandana: *Talk to her in the morning.*

She and Megan are having a good moment right now.

Quincy: *Got it. Thanks.*

Mandana: *Good night.*

Quincy: *Good night.*

It was a really good night. Especially our kiss. I would like to do a lot more kissing. Quincy could almost feel the heat of Mandana's lips, the strength of her hands, the powerful thrust and parry of her tongue as his own hands slid into his underwear.

Thursday morning, Quincy woke up feeling refreshed, horny, and a bit guilty. He sent a quick text to Tasha to ensure they had a chance to talk when they dropped their kids off at school. Quincy fed Dolly, helped get Ruby ready, and was somewhat presentable himself by the time they left.

Once the girls were inside the school, Tasha asked, "What's up, Que Tee?"

Quincy groaned, "I really hoped that nickname would die."

Tasha mock pouted. "Fine. We'll retire it."

"Thank you."

"Have you ever considered shaving your head?"

"Why?" Quincy cocked a quizzical eyebrow at her.

"Q Ball would be a fun nickname."

He sighed. "You're killing me. Seriously, though, can you watch Ruby today?"

"Let me guess, you and Mandana have to talk about the kiss, right?"

"You know? Of course, you know. Are there no secrets at all?"

Tasha shrugged. "Yes, but selective. Mandana called Megan last night for some friendly advice."

"What did she say?"

Tasha tut-tutted him. "Selective secrets, remember."

"Oh, *now* we're keeping secrets? Are you serious?"

"Girl code. Sorry."

"You're killing me. Absolutely killing me. Can you tell me anything at all? I'll share my secrets with you."

Tasha's laughter drew a scowl from Rachel as she dropped off her boys. When she finally stopped laughing, Tasha responded, "You're adorable. You think you have secrets. *Wow.* You're funny."

At least when I get home, I will finally be the smartest one in the room. Then again, there's a decent chance Dolly Purrton is more intelligent than me, too. She gets free food, scratchings, and cuddles. Dammit.

Tasha continued, "I'm going to tell you what I told Mandana. When you talk to her, be honest. I mean completely honest."

"I can be honest."

She gave Mandana advice? Some secrets do slip out.

Tasha gave him an affectionate pat on the cheek. "Why don't I pick the girls up after school and watch them until you and Mandana talk about what you need to talk about?"

"Perfect. Thanks, Tasha."

"You're welcome. Remember what I said, and don't screw this up, Quincy."

"I will. I won't. You know what I mean. Have a good day."

"You too." She gave him a saucy wink and a flirty wave as she turned to leave. He could feel Rachel's glare on his back as he walked toward home.

I hope things work out for Rachel and her husband. I should probably ask Tasha not to tease her. Or at least not too much. One thing is for sure: Whatever connection I had with Rachel is nothing next to what I feel about Mandana. Tasha is right, I better not screw this up. Speaking of not screwing this up, I should text Mandana.

Quincy: *We said we would talk about last night.*

I think in person would be better.

Mandana: *Yes.*

Can I come over after you are done with work?

Do I agree to this? My place is so...cheap, especially compared to hers. Fuck it. Tasha said to be honest. If she can't deal with it, then I need to find out now.

Quincy: *Come over around four?*

Mandana: *CU then.*

The apartment wasn't too dirty; however, Quincy did some light cleaning to make it more presentable. By about four o'clock, when Mandana texted to ask for a coffee order, Quincy's apartment looked lived-in but presentable. She showed up fifteen minutes later, bearing a hot beverage in each hand. Mandana handed him a cup as he ushered her in.

"*Oh, hi.* Who is this little charmer?"

"This is Dolly Purrton."

Mandana snickered. "Let me guess, you named her."

"I did."

"I like the name, and she is a little cutie."

"Would you like to sit at the table or on the couch? I'm sorry my place isn't as nice as yours."

"Quincy, you're a single father who has been focused on raising a wonderful daughter on one income. I'm...I'm operating under a whole different set of circumstances. I like your place. I feel like you've made a good home for Ruby. As for where to sit, let's sit on the couch."

Way to go, Quincy. You almost managed to blow it in the first thirty seconds. Wow, I've never seen her in jeans and a sweater before. It is definitely hotter than the dresses and skirts.

"Sure. Um. How was your day?"

"My day has been busy and productive, but we aren't here to talk about our days, are we?"

He took a deep breath. "No. I guess we aren't. Mandana, I have something to confess."

"What is it?"

"I am scared shitless right now. Absolutely terrified."

"Why?"

"Because I feel like the next few minutes are potentially going to make or break whatever this is between us, and I really don't want to fuck it up."

Mandana breathed a sigh of relief. "Whew. Okay, I feel the same way, too."

His sigh matched hers. "You do?"

"Yes."

They smiled at each other and took nervous sips of their drinks.

"Once more unto the breach, dear friends." Henry the Something. Shakespeare sounds about right for whatever is about to happen. Here goes...everything.

"Mandana, I know we had a deal when we started this whole fake dating, fake fiancée thing. I feel like I have violated—" Quincy paused to take a deep breath. "—All of it, honestly. If not in letter, then in spirit."

I wish I were good at reading people's emotions. Is my revelation a good thing or a bad thing?

"We agreed to no feelings and no strings, and now I suddenly find myself bound in a web of emotions. I understand if you want to end our deal, but I have to tell you I have...feelings for you. Strong feelings."

There was a pause, an interminable pause, before Mandana spoke. "I do want to end our deal."

Fuck, I blew it.

"I want to end our deal because I also have strong feelings for you. I've also grown very fond of Ruby."

"Wait. Sorry, I'm trying to catch up here. When you say you want to end our deal, do you mean—"

"Quincy, it means I want whatever this is between us to be real, but we need to be sure we are right for each other. If we aren't, then we can go back to the deal. My highest priority is ensuring you and Ruby stay together. The next highest priority is making sure that Stacy bitch goes home empty-handed."

"I agree."

"Good. I need to know something, and I need you to be completely honest with me."

"Of course."

"When you said you would only want more kids under a few limited circumstances, were you being honest?"

"Yes, why? Do you want to have kids of your own?"

"No. A long time ago, I decided motherhood wasn't for me. It took me nine doctors, but I finally found one who would tie my tubes."

"Why did it take you nine doctors?"

"Because eight of them said I was too young and should wait in case I wanted to have kids with some future husband. So, they put some future I didn't want ahead of what I actually wanted them to do," Mandana snarled.

"*Damn.* That's fucked up."

"Tell me about it."

"Sorry, let's rewind. You said motherhood wasn't for you, but I have Ruby."

Mandana reached out to gently touch his arm. "Ruby is a treasure. I talked with Tasha because she's in a similar situation, and I am starting to like the idea of..."

"Yes?"

"Sorry. I'm struggling to find the right words. I want to read to her at night, help her with her homework, or watch her skate in roller derby. I'm not asking to be her mom because, for better or worse, she has one of those already. I'm trying to say that I would like to be part of her life in whatever way works for her and you."

"I think she would love having you in our lives. Ruby set us up last night. You know that, right?"

"Megan explained it to me. I'm honestly extremely impressed. It's possible Sophia was an accomplice. I had no idea little kids could be so cunning."

He grinned. "Parenthood is one revelation after another, *trust me*."

"Is it weird I'm looking forward to finding out more?"

Quincy couldn't help but chortle. "Yes, yes, it is. Any other major things to discuss?"

"There is one other thing."

"What is it?"

"Money."

"Oh. I'm not rich or anything—"

Mandana cut him off. "I am."

"I figured you were doing okay for yourself based on your apartment. Like, how rich are we talking about here?"

"Not stupid rich. Comfortable. I was a high-end bartender in Manhattan for about three years. I listened to a lot of drunk hedge fund bros and figured out pretty quickly who was stupid and who wasn't. I made some good money based on drunken conversation. Plus, Wall Street guys dropped tens of thousands of dollars on booze, so the tips were *phenomenal*. And if you think the hedge fund bros dropped money, when the oil sheiks came in, they sometimes ran up bar tabs in the hundreds of thousands. I lived frugally and invested a lot. From there, it was off to Miami. The high rollers changed a bit, but I raked in a shitload of cash. I hit Vegas, and that was okay, but then COVID hit. So, back to Miami, which was risky, but the money was stupidly good. Then LA once everything went back to normal."

"Wow, so you made a ton of money."

"Yeah, and then my car broke down in Portland, and I loved it here so much that I moved. The money isn't as good, but I don't give a shit. Mostly thanks to my brother, Cyrus."

"How so?"

"Remember when I told you some Wall Street guys are smart, and others are idiots? Well, Cyrus is an idiot. He was all-in on crypto from the start."

"I never figured out crypto."

"Don't bother. Anyway, not long after Bitcoin launched, he gave me one thousand of them, which was worth one hundred bucks at the time. 'This is the future,' he said. As I figured, Bitcoin has never become a real alternate currency, although the black market loves it. Anyway, it went up and down, but I didn't pay much attention because I was doing well without it. So, a few years ago, Bitcoin spiked, and I told myself I'd sell it all when it hit fifty grand. Instead, it stalls at forty and crashes...again. Then, during the pandemic, it spikes. I sold all thousand of them at fifty thousand dollars each. The spike went until sixty and then crashed again. Making stupid bets against massive volatility is why Cyrus isn't allowed near investments anymore."

Quincy whispered in awe, "You made fifty million dollars."

"Minus taxes."

"Holy shit."

"Thus, I'm pouring a shitload of money into a cat cafe. Honestly, I think it can be a great business, but if it isn't, then I'm still okay."

"Did you tell me this because you thought I wouldn't like you?"

"No, I told you this because if we go all the way, you're going to sign a prenup."

Business Mandana is cold but still so sexy.

Quincy nodded. "I can live with a prenup." A sly grin crept across his face. "Speaking of all the way, does the end of our deal mean the whole platonic restriction is off the table because I really enjoyed our kiss last night."

Quincy watched as Mandana's expression morphed from ice-cold businesswoman to sultry sex kitten. "I thought about kissing you a lot last night. I mean *a lot*." She leaned in toward him like a hunting lioness.

"Me, too."

"How much did you think about kissing me?" Her fingers toyed with his shirt's top button.

"Um."

"Be honest." The top button slipped open, and fingernails scraped down to the next.

"I...I can't believe I'm about to admit this." Quincy's face turned beet red. "I touched myself."

"Mmmm, did you flog your bishop? Beat your meat?" Another button is gone.

"Yes," he whispered, embarrassment turning to excitement.

"Yes, what? Say it, or I stop."

"I polished my knob." His shirt was half undone now, and those fingertips continued to scrape delicately southward to the next button.

Mandana purred, "*Good boy*. You're so hot."

"Did you?"

"Did I what?"

"You know…"

"Say it, Quincy. Say it or I'll stop," Mandana growled.

"Did you shuck your oyster?"

Mandana's hair brushed against his mostly bare chest as she convulsed with laughter. "Shuck my oyster? I've never heard that euphemism before. I love it. And to answer your question, yes, I gilded my lily last night."

The angle of Mandana's head shifted, and her tongue traced the outline of Quincy's nipple. Those relentless fingers were now releasing the final button. Mandana backed off.

"Are you good with this? I don't want to do anything you are uncomfortable with."

"I'm good. Very good. And the same for you. Just tell me if I am near or past your limits."

"Communication, I like it. I wore skin-tight jeans, so my pants stayed on. You get no further until you get tested. I still remember your fun time with Sara."

"Um, I'll get tested immediately."

"In the immortal words of Salt-N-Pepa, you better make it fast, or else I'm gonna be pissed."

"Oh, I will. I really want to push it. Push it real good."

She moaned, "Fuck, you're sexy." Mandana yanked his shirt off and planted her lips on his, forcing him backward against the arm of the couch. As their tongues wrestled, Quincy slid his hands under her plum sweater. Starting at her hips, he traced back to her spine and up. He felt Mandana's back arch as she reacted to the leisurely advance of his fingertips.

Quincy pulled back from the kiss once his fingers reached her shoulder blades. "May I?" Mandana nodded, and he drew the sweater up and over her head. "Holy shit, you are gorgeous."

"Thank you. I like my view as well."

Her red bra against her bronze skin is stunning.

She straddled him and latched her mouth onto one of his earlobes in a frenzy of nibbling and sucking. Mandana's hot breath blasted in Quincy's ear as she whispered huskily, "Take my fucking bra off." Not one to refuse a lady, Quincy reached behind with one hand and popped the clasp. "Mmmm, someone has skills." The two of them wrestled the bra off, a task made more difficult by Mandana's refusal to stop attacking Quincy's ear.

They both sighed as bare skin touched bare skin. Quincy took this opportunity to grab a fistful of Mandana's hair at the nape of her neck and pull her off his ear.

"Is this okay?"

"Oh, fuck yes."

With her consent confirmed, Quincy pulled her lips back to his. The firm pressure of his fist in her hair seemed to drive Mandana into passionate madness. Quincy winced as her nails dug into his back.

Her breasts felt incredible as they pressed into his chest. He released his hold on her hair and moved his hands to the front to better feel her firm bust. Quincy quivered in excitement when he heard Mandana's throaty moan when his thumbs touched her nipples. She mewled softly as his fingers caressed the soft undersides of her breasts.

"Do you like my tits?"

"A bit," Quincy said coyly.

"Tease. I need you to twist my nipples a bit. Not too much. Perfect. Oh, fuck. Oh, Goddess. Keep doing what you're doing. Now get your fucking tongue back in my mouth."

She tells me what she wants, yet she also likes to have me yank her hair. Awesome. She feels incredible. Wait...what's happening...

Quincy felt his head yanked back by Mandana's grasp on the back of his neck. She rose up and forced his mouth onto one nipple. "Teeth, just a bit. Keep your other hand going. A little more teeth. Fuck, yes. Get your other hand on my ass. Oh, Goddess. Nip my boobs *lightly*. If I see a bite mark tonight, you're going to pay. Perfect. Fucking hell, Quincy, you're hitting the right spots. Suck me now. And some tongue. Holy goddess, I am fucking drenched right now."

Quincy rode Mandana's stream of consciousness, hanging on for dear life as she bucked and writhed beneath his touch. With a lurch, she dropped to straddle one of his legs, keeping his mouth firmly attached to her nipple while she ground on his thigh. The feel of her wetness rocking on him sent shivers of excitement rocketing up his spine.

Thinking quickly, Quincy took his right hand off of one breast to grab the back of the couch and moved his left hand from her ass to her saliva-coated right boob. Thus braced, Quincy continued his ministrations as Mandana thrashed on his thigh. She dropped one of her hands down to keep herself steady. Quincy was fully aware of just how close her fingers were to his engorged cock. As much as he craved her touch, his focus remained entirely on her pleasure. Suddenly, with a shuddering cry, she collapsed and fell limply forward.

He held her sweaty and panting form against his chest. Quincy listened to Mandana's joyful whimpers and felt her quivering after-shocks. He gently stroked her matted hair with his free hand.

Now is probably not the best time to speak. If her hand moves even a tiny bit, I'm pretty sure I'm going to explode. I just need to breathe because I'd feel weird if I dumped a load in my underwear right now. Let me hold her, and she'll talk when she is ready. I'm pretty sure I've never brought anyone to orgasm with my leg before.

"Hi," Mandana uttered weakly.

"Hi. Do you feel good?"

Mandana's only answer was to purr and gently stroke his cheek. "Quincy?"

"Yes."

"Do you mind if I am vocal and demanding?"

"No. Not at all." Quincy paused to think. "Actually, I like it. You take the guesswork out of things. I don't think I have ever nipped someone's boobs before. Nipples a bit, but not the rest. I enjoyed exploring new things, don't get me wrong."

"Okay. Good. There's one other thing I need to tell you."

"Go for it."

"If we go all the way, then you need to know I can't cum without clitoral stimulation."

"So, you need a finger, thumb, vibrator, or my entire thigh to stimulate you. Got it."

"You don't think it's weird?" She asked shyly.

"Statistically, it makes you normal." He flashed her a grin. "I've been doing some reading and reflecting since our first date slash interview."

Mandana melted. "Aw, you remembered our talk."

"I'm not likely to forget it. Has anyone ever told you how fierce you are?"

"Probably, but I like hearing it from you. Quincy, I'm sorry I didn't take care of your needs."

"You don't need to apologize. Let's promise not to get caught up in the reciprocity trap. If I can be honest, I nearly creamed my underwear. Trust me, I will have plenty of ammunition for later when I have my date with Rosy Palmer and her five friends."

"Thank you for being considerate. Also, thank you for not running away at dinner last night. Persian-style seating was a huge test, and you passed with flying colors."

"Any other tests I should know about?"

Mandana mused for a minute before asking, "Do you do any manscaping?"

Quincy choked. "There's a question I wasn't expecting. When I was with Rachel, she suggested sugaring, and I've been getting my hair ripped out for a few months now."

"Nice. Full-on Brazilian?"

Quincy blushed. "Yes. Less maintenance."

Mandana grinned. "Good choice."

"Thanks. Anything else?"

"Just your STD panel."

"I'll get right on it."

"That's what she said," were Mandana's last words before she drifted off to sleep.

I'm good with being like this.

Chapter 18

Love Again

Dua Lipa

Mandana woke up with her head resting on Quincy's bare chest. She could feel his heart beating underneath her ear. One of his hands made lazy twirls in her hair while his other arm was draped warmly across her. Quincy's breath was warm in her hair.

This feels so good. Comfortable. Oh, probably not for him.

"I'm sorry, Quincy. This can't be comfortable for you."

"Well, I'm getting a bit of a cramp, but I don't want you to move." With a little laugh, he added, "Ever."

"You're not worried about your legs falling off?"

He frowned in mock contemplation before answering, "Slightly, but it would be a price worth paying to keep you in my arms."

"Flatterer." She blew a raspberry at him. "How long was I out?"

"About fifteen minutes."

Whatever thing he is doing with my hair feels fantastic.

"If you want to adjust how you are sitting, please do so. I'll go back to pressing my boobs against you again once you're comfortable."

Quincy groaned and shifted. Mandana lifted up to allow him to move. He sighed as he settled into a sitting position with his back against the corner of the couch.

"Wait a sec," Quincy said before she could move.

"Do you need to stretch?"

"Oh, great idea. First, I just wanted a chance to admire you."

Way to tell a girl what she likes to hear. Let's give him a show.

Mandana knelt on the couch with her back straight. She watched Quincy's eyes as they roamed freely, his expression hungry. Mandana asked coyly, "Is this what you wanted to admire?" She added a subtle arch to her back, making her breasts more prominent.

"You are incredibly beautiful."

"Thank you. Am I okay to cuddle with you now?"

"Yes, please."

A man who wants to cuddle? Sign me up.

Mandana worked herself next to Quincy, melding herself against him. "You feel perfect."

"So do you." He took hold of her hand. His hand felt warm and strong.

"You aren't going to feel my tits?"

"Do you want me to?"

"Actually, I really enjoy holding your hand like this. I think I'm mostly impressed you went for my hand first. You're a good person, Quincy. I like that about you. You do have my permission to feel them, but only if you want to."

"Thank you. I will definitely take you up on your offer sometime. Right now, I really want to kiss you."

Put a ring on my finger now, you sensitive stud.

Wordlessly, Mandana leaned in to kiss Quincy. Their tongues no longer wrestled feverishly. Instead, they engaged in a slow, sensual tango. Once again, Quincy's hand twirled intricate patterns in her hair. She melted in his arms as their passion smoldered.

A buzzing phone broke their intimate spell. Quincy gently pushed her back.

"We don't have to check our phones," Mandana purred.

"You might not, but I have to in case it's Ruby."

Something I should think about as well.

Quincy continued, "It is Ruby. Megan is making stir fry tonight. She wants to know if I want to have dinner with them."

"Oh. Her stir fry should be delicious."

His head bobbed in agreement. "Yeah. Megan is a great cook."

"So, I guess you are going then?"

"I am." She watched a slow grin develop on his face. "I'll ask if I can bring a plus one."

"Are you sure about this? I feel like—" Mandana looked Quincy straight in the eyes. "If we go over there together, then we're announcing this thing between us is real."

Quincy paused momentarily before responding, "I feel like they already assume we are, but I don't want you to feel pressured into doing this if you aren't comfortable."

I can't believe just how comfortable I feel.

"Let's do this. I just wanted to be sure."

Quincy's boyish grime morphed into a beaming smile. She watched him text Ruby, and they both waited expectantly for the response. Quincy's phone buzzed again, and he read Ruby's text aloud. "She says, 'Is Miss Mandana coming?'"

Before Mandana could answer, her own phone buzzed. "It's Megan. She wants to know if I'm with you. I'll tell her yes. She wants to know how much time we need."

"How much time do we need?"

"Well, how long does it take to get to their place?"

"About ten minutes walking or two minutes driving. Walking is probably better."

"Good to know. Let me think. Fifteen minutes of making out, five minutes to dress and touch up my makeup and hair—"

He raised his eyebrows. "Um."

Mandana felt a touch of panic. "What? How bad is my makeup and hair?"

Quincy smirked like a naughty schoolboy. "Let me preface my response by saying you look so fucking sexy right now; however, your makeup and hair do look like you recently had an orgasm."

"Thank you for your honest assessment. All right, five minutes of making out—" She agreed with Quincy's groan of disappointment. "—then fifteen minutes to get dressed and fix my makeup and hair, then ten minutes to walk over. So, I'll say thirty minutes."

"We should get started, then."

"Let me set a timer."

Quincy's whimper was adorable.

"Timer set. You have five minutes in heaven, lover boy."

Ten minutes later, Mandana was leaning heavily against the bathroom counter to steady her shaking legs as she vainly tried to fix her hair.

Well, he definitely made good use of those five minutes. And a couple of bonus minutes. My toys are getting a workout tonight. Whoever figured out how to make waterproof, rechargeable vibrators deserves a Nobel Prize.

When Mandana emerged from the bathroom, she was met by a wolf whistle from Quincy, who was sitting on the couch with a very happy Dolly Purrton in his lap.

"Mandana, I don't mean to criticize, but your makeup is still a bit...you still look like you recently orgasmed."

"It's *your* fucking fault. My hands and legs won't stop quivering." She tried to sound angry, but they both knew it was a façade. "Dammit, Quincy, wipe your proud smile off of your face. Actually, don't; you kinda deserve it. You really did make me feel good. Also, do you plan to put on a shirt?"

"I mean, I would—" Quincy gestured to the happy feline. "—but I'm having some trouble."

"Let me pet the cat while you put a shirt on."

"Thanks."

Dolly Purrton chirped in dismay at being disturbed but consented to Mandana's petting.

"Bye, Dolly," Mandana said as they left. "Is it stupid to say goodbye to a cat?"

"Nah, I do it all the time."

"Good to know."

They walked hand in hand over to Megan and Tasha's home. Tasha met them at the door. "Before we go up, I just want to clarify that this is real, right?"

Quincy beat Mandana to the answer, affirming, "Yes, it is."

"Good. Quincy, you go on up. I need to help Mandana out for a minute."

"Um, sure. See you up there."

Once he was out of sight, Tasha said, "Girl, we need a minute to fix your makeup because you can't go in there looking like you just got fucked silly."

"I tried, but my hands weren't working right," Mandana complained. "Also, we didn't go all the way."

"Yet..."

"Okay, yet. But he did make me cum."

Tasha beamed triumphantly. "Hand me your makeup. Did you make him cum?"

"No. I feel bad. A thank you hand job would have been appropriate."

The other woman shrugged. "Yeah, but also sorta disappointing."

Mandana whispered, "I can't believe I'm standing in the entryway talking about hand jobs while you fix my makeup. Speaking of, how does my hair look?"

"You did your best. Thankfully, Megan is a smart woman, and she sent me down here with an extra hair tie. Do you want a high ponytail or low?"

"High, please."

"Good call. Has anyone told you that you have a fantastic neck?"

"No, but thank you."

"Turn around. I'll get your hair."

"Thanks, Tasha."

"Okay, let me see. Oh, shit." Tasha gawked at her. "You need to do this messy high ponytail thing more often. Once Megan grows her hair out more, she is definitely going to be rocking the messy pony look. A lot."

Mandana brushed at the stray locks of hair framing her face, grabbing one and holding it out. "This is a good look for me?"

"Trust me, it's a fucking great look," Tasha said through gritted teeth.

"All right. I'm not big on stray hair, especially where I work. Given your visceral reaction, I'll keep this in mind."

"You should. Come on, let's go up."

Once in the apartment, Megan leered at her from the kitchen. "Hi, Mandana. Come here and help me out. Tasha, please be a dear and keep Quincy and the girls company."

Mandana gave her friend a side hug. "Hey, Megan. Can I help you?"

"Nope. The girls did most of the work. I just need to throw everything together now, but I wanted to talk first. I'm assuming things are going well with Quincy."

"They are. We decided this whole fake thing wasn't working for either of us."

"How do you feel about this?"

"I'm really happy, Megan. I like him a lot. Ruby is a special kid."

"Talking with Tasha was helpful, then?"

"It was. Did you two plan this?"

"I wish. No, Tasha just felt in the moment that it was something you might need to hear. She's really intuitive." Megan sighed longingly.

"You two really are special. As individuals and as a couple. It's aspirational."

Megan's smile was infectious. "Would you like some advice?"

"Please."

"Enjoy the physical, which you clearly are."

Mandana nodded.

Megan continued, "But concentrate on the emotional aspects. Combine the two to strengthen your bond. Last night, after your call, you're probably thinking Tasha and I went at it."

"Yeah, you sounded kinda worked up."

"I was, emotionally. We just held each other and talked. You're a big girl, so I assume you can handle a little TMI. Skin-to-skin contact while building our emotional bond is amazing and important. Last night, we were naked both physically and emotionally. It wasn't sex. It was love. I never had anywhere near that kind of emotional intimacy with my ex-husband."

"That's powerful."

"It's very fucking powerful. Trust me, sex with Tasha is incredible, but I can't begin to describe just how amazing it can feel to simply be with her."

"Aw. Can I hug you again?"

"Of course."

"Thank you, Megan. I appreciate you talking with me. If I'm being honest, I think about why I've been single for the past few years. I couldn't find what you were talking about. Eventually, I just stopped looking."

Megan looked stunned. "Mandana, did you say years?"

"Yeah. I got tired of guys who weren't willing to take the time to understand me and certainly didn't care about my needs. Eventually, I decided if I was going just to have to get myself off anyway, then I might as well not risk diseases and stick with silicone."

"Wow. That sucks. I'm really sorry."

"Thanks."

"You think Quincy is different?"

"Yeah. He definitely needs some training, but most men do. I feel like he's an incredible guy, and we seem to be connecting emotionally."

Megan gave her another hug. "Oh, Mandana, you've got it bad. I'm so happy for you."

Yeah, I do have it bad. Like L-word bad.

"I'm happy, too."

"Aw." Mandana felt Megan give her a friendly kiss on the cheek before breaking their embrace. "Okay, can you go and get the girls? It's time for me to show them how to put this all together."

"Sure. Megan, has anyone ever told you that you are a great hugger and a great mom?"

Megan's laugh practically sparkled. "Tasha does. I don't get tired of hearing it."

Mandana walked into the living area and summoned the girls, who raced into the kitchen. Quincy stood, saying, "I want to watch as well. Apparently, my culinary skills need some improvement." He followed her back to observe Megan at work. Mandana took this opportunity to slide in front of him and press herself back, wrapping his arms around her. Checking in, she asked, "Is this okay? I mean, in front of Ruby?"

Ruby might not even notice us. Nope, she saw us. She smiled at us. Wow, her approval makes me feel warm and gooey all over.

"I'm good with it, and I think she might have just given us her blessing."

"I think she did. That makes me happy. Quincy, I—"

Love you. Shit, I can't say the L-word. At least, not yet.

"—I feel really comfortable with you."

He whispered softly in her ear. "Me, too. I love...how you feel in my arms."

Did he almost say he loves me?

Mandana pressed backward against him. "Good, I'll stay right here then." They stood there in silence, observing Megan demon-strate how to make stir fry to the two girls. The wok sizzled and popped, filling the air with delicious smells as Megan stirred furiously. Ruby and Sophia broke into applause as Megan hefted the wok, declaring that dinner was ready. Mandana broke free with a languorous sigh and sat down next to Quincy. She was surprised when Ruby chose to sit on her other side and even more surprised when Ruby gave her hand a little squeeze.

Ruby beckoned her to lean over, and Mandana complied. "Thank you for making Daddy smile. I think he loves you," Ruby whispered in her ear.

Mandana turned and whispered back, "Can you keep a secret?"

She nodded, "Yes, Miss Mandana."

"You can't tell him, but I think I love him, too."

I just said those words out loud. Not to him, but I said them. I can't remember the last time I said those words.

Ruby interrupted her reverie, stating, "I really like you, too."

Mandana smiled, "You are a very special girl, *azizam*."

"What does *azizam* mean?"

"It translates to 'my dear' in Farsi, the language of Persia."

"Ooh, I like it."

Mandana squeezed Ruby's hand before sitting up.

Quincy asked, "What were you two talking about?"

"Girl talk. None of your business," she responded airily. Mandana gave him a dazzling smile and a saucy wink. Quincy shook his head in the world-weary way known to men all over.

Chapter 19

Long Cool Woman (In a Black Dress)

The Hollies

Friday passed in a blur of activity. Quincy went to get tested for STIs. He found it more difficult and uncomfortable to walk in the door than it was to get the actual tests. The workday ended right as he needed to walk to pick up Ruby and Sophia, so he spent the afternoon with the girls. They drank tea, read books, and petted Dolly Purrton. Dolly wandered from lap to lap, purring happily. The girls helped him bake cookies from scratch, which was a first for him.

Around six thirty, Tasha stopped by to talk about freelance work before taking Sophia home. After they finished talking shop, Tasha asked, "How are you feeling?"

"There's a lot to unpack with your question. In general, I am very anxious. Tomorrow's meeting with Stacy terrifies me. I haven't seen her since Ruby was born, and I have no idea what she is like. Honestly, I don't even know what she was like before Ruby was born because we were high all the time." Quincy sighed heavily. "Right, there's another feeling, shame. I'm ashamed I had a child with a woman I didn't even know. I don't regret it at all because Ruby is amazing. So yeah, there's a lot going on in my head right now."

"But there's some good stuff, too, right?"

"Yeah. I'm feeling terrific about things with Mandana right now. Thinking of her is keeping me in a good place. She and these two little angels. Oh, would you like a chocolate chip cookie? They helped me bake some this afternoon."

Tasha gave him a cheery smile. "You're very proud, aren't you?"

Quincy looked at her sheepishly. "It was my first time baking cookies from scratch."

"Aw, you should be proud. I won't tell you not to worry about tomorrow because we both know you'll worry. Instead, I will remind you that you will be surrounded by people who support you."

"Thank you, Tasha."

Tasha got Sophia bundled up, and they headed out. "See you tomorrow, Quincy. The cookies are delicious."

Quincy didn't sleep well, nor did Ruby, which made for a rough morning. They were irritable and snappy as they had breakfast and did some Saturday morning chores. Tasha invited them over for lunch, which proved to be a relief for parents and children.

Arriving at Tasha's about thirty minutes later, Ruby immediately ran to see Sophia while Quincy joined Tasha in the kitchen. "You look a bit rough," Tasha commented.

"Yeah. I slept like ass. Ruby didn't sleep well, either. We are both really wound up about this, although probably for different reasons."

"Megan and Mandana will be here soon. Super Mom can take care of Ruby and help get her sorted out. I'll let Mandana help calm you down."

"What will you be doing?"

"Supervising, of course." Tasha chuckled.

Quincy heard the door open behind him and turned to greet the newcomers.

"Hi, Megan, and hi, Mandana."

"Hey, Quincy. I didn't expect to see you until later." Megan looked surprised but pleased.

"Yeah, I figured he might be nervous. Love, can you check on Ruby? I think she might need your maternal support."

"On it."

Mandana directed a warm smile at him. "Hi, Quincy. How are you?"

"Closing in on a nervous wreck."

"Go sit down at the table and turn sideways on a chair. I'll take good care of you," Mandana directed. "Tasha, you good?"

"All good. Go help out your man." Quincy caught the lewd wink Tasha leveled at her.

She came up behind him, and he felt her fingernails trace slowly across his back. With both hands, Mandana scratched up and down his back with slow and gentle strokes. Quincy groaned longingly at the exquisite feelings her fingers evoked. He whimpered when her hands moved to his head, twisting and twirling through his hair to caress his scalp.

This feels amazing. She could do this forever, and I would be happy.

Mandana's fingernails returned to his back, which arched and undulated under her delicate touch. Her breath was warm in his ear as her fingertips grazed the small of his back. "You look like you are enjoying this," she purred in his ears.

"Mmmm Hmmm."

"Do you like this gentle pressure? Can you imagine how it would feel on your bare skin? I'll do this for you another time when we can take this shirt off. Would you like that?"

"Mmmm Hmmm."

"I like doing this for you. Would you like to do this for me sometime?" Quincy nodded as Mandana continued. "I want you to know I will be right beside you today. You and Ruby have my complete and total support. I know this is going to be very hard for you, but we will get through this together. We are all here to support you and Ruby." Her voice was soft and comforting.

Quincy eventually found his own voice again. "Thank you, Mandana."

"Do you need more back-scratching?"

"I don't think I will ever say 'no' to more, but right now, would you be willing to sit in my lap and hug me?"

"Sure, baby. Anything you need."

Quincy turned in the chair as Mandana walked around him and delicately sat down, twisting and running her arms around his shoulders. His arms encircled her midriff as she lay her head down on his shoulder. An intoxicating mixture of citrus, lavender, and sweat filled Quincy's nostrils, a scent he was beginning to associate with Mandana.

"Thank you," he whispered.

"Are you better?"

"Yes. Much better."

"Good. I'm glad to hear it. I'm going to get changed."

Quincy's hands lingered as Mandana levered herself into a standing position. He was acutely aware of how her yoga clothes were almost painted onto her body. Mandana gave him a lecherous smile as she bent down to whisper in his ear, "Before I get changed, I need to peel off these hot and sweaty clothes. Then, I'm going to take a steamy shower. I'll feel so alone in there without you. I might even touch myself while I imagine you joining me, our bodies slick and wet under the running water. Quincy, I'm already soaking wet just thinking about it. Mmmm."

Mandana quickly stood up and cheerily exclaimed, "Okay, I'm gonna shower now. Tasha, thank you for letting me borrow your bathroom." Then she was gone, pausing just before she entered the primary bedroom to give a stunned Quincy a wave and a sultry wink.

Holy shit, she is going to kill me. What a way to die, though.

"I have no idea what she said to you, but you seem to be in a better mood." Quincy had almost forgotten about everything else and was startled by Tasha's voice.

"Oh, yes. I'm feeling much better."

"I would ask you to set the table, but I suspect you might need a minute before you can stand up." Quincy felt blood rush into his cheeks at her words.

"Yeah, I definitely need a minute."

"Take your time, sugar."

Once lunch was ready, Megan and Quincy ate with the girls while Tasha went to help Mandana get ready. After she finished eating, Megan excused herself so she could get ready, leaving Quincy with the girls.

"Ruby, I am sorry I was snappy with you earlier."

"It's okay, Daddy! I'm anxious about seeing Mom, too."

"I know. I haven't seen your mother since a couple of days after you were born. I haven't heard from her in years. I'm very anxious. I really hope this meeting goes well."

"Me, too."

"I'm glad you will finally get to meet her."

"What do you think she will be like, Daddy?"

Quincy paused before responding. "I honestly don't know. We were both very young when you were born, and we—"

How do I say this?

"We made a lot of mistakes when we were together. One of those mistakes was that we didn't communicate well. We really didn't know each other. So, when you were born, I think your mom was very scared. I know because I was scared, too. We each handled your arrival in different ways. I'm not angry with your mom for the choice she made, and I hope you aren't, either."

"I'm not mad."

"Good. The most important thing I want you to know is that while I made a lot of mistakes, you aren't one of them."

"Thank you, Daddy."

"You're adorable." Quincy whipped his head around to see who spoke. He hadn't noticed Mandana and Tasha's entrance while he was talking with Ruby.

"I...wow."

Mandana grinned triumphantly and twirled around. "I take it you approve?"

"Approve is an understatement," he blurted.

"Girls, why don't you go and read on the couch?" Tasha reached out and gently lifted Quincy's chin to close his gaping mouth. "Miss Mandana and I need to eat while Miss Megan gets ready."

Ruby and Sophia sprinted off. Tasha sat and served herself some penne before saying, "Mandana, please sit and eat. I think you broke Quincy again."

"I'm not broken."

"Coulda fooled me with your mouth open like you're catching flies."

"In my defense, Mandana is stunning."

Tasha's whisper to Mandana was pitched so Quincy could easily hear it. "You would think this poor boy had never seen a woman before."

Mandana tittered before replying, "Tasha, stop teasing him."

"Fine. It's fun, though."

"Can I ask why you are so dressed up for Powell's?"

"Oh, sweetie. I'm not dressed up for Powell's. I'm dressed up for your ex."

"Quincy, Mandana is making what you might call a power play. When this Stacy woman shows up, she is going to see a smoking hot Mandana on your arm. She is going to be immediately outclassed by this stunning, brilliant woman who speaks three languages, and she's going to know it."

"Four. I speak four languages."

"What's the fourth?"

"I'm fluent in English, Farsi, and Spanish. My Arabic is rusty, but I'm confident I can hold my own."

"Damn, girl. You are sexy. Anyway, like I was saying...Mandana is obviously a step up—probably a whole flight of stairs up—from this Stacy person."

I suddenly feel like a guy who brought a wooden spoon to a knife fight.

"Speaking of...Tasha, should I wear the jacket or not?"

"Hmmm, unless it's super cold in there, don't wear the jacket. Your black biker jacket is badass, but your tattoos are even more badass. Quincy, what do you think?"

I think maybe it's not a wooden spoon. Probably a spork.

"Ummm. Jacket off?"

"All right, no jacket, then. Speaking of badass tattoos, I've been inspired by your panther tattoo on your thigh, Tasha. I'm working with someone to design a thigh tattoo for me."

"What's the idea?"

"My sleeve has all this ancient Persian imagery, right? So, what I'm thinking is sort of an extension for the thigh, but the centerpiece of the design will be my namesake, Queen Mandana, standing at the gates of a city, surrounded by flame motifs and winged lions. I have a preliminary sketch on my phone. Take a look." Mandana pulled out her phone to show them.

"Wow, that's awesome. Quincy, you need some tattoos."

"I dunno..."

"Mandana and I will help you. Oh...I have the best idea. Mandana and I will take you and Megan to get inked."

Quincy nodded. "Maybe. No tramp stamps, though." Mandana and Tasha exchanged triumphant smiles. "Um. So, why this particular outfit?"

Mandana looked exceptionally pleased with his question. "Starting from the top. Tasha put my hair in this stylishly messy bun in a deliberate way to suggest I mean business but can have fun. My makeup, including the scarlet lipstick, does the same thing. The vest matches the lipstick and is a powerful color that works really well with my skin tone. Further down, the black skirt works well with the vest. It's also business-like and sexy, especially with the side slit. When my legs are positioned just right, the skirt shows a hint of the black stockings underneath. The knee-high black boots with gold buckles tie the whole look together."

At a loss for words, Quincy managed to say, "I put on jeans and a nice shirt."

Mandana kissed him. "Quincy, I adore your innocence."

Yep. I brought a spork to a sword fight.

Chapter 20

Modern Day Cowboy

Tesla

Mandana stood coolly in the Burnside lobby of Powell's, her arm through Quincy's in a manner simultaneously casual and possessive. Stacy and her husband were late, and Mandana felt Quincy's blood pressure rising.

She took a quick glance over at Megan and Tasha, who were carefully shepherding Ruby and Sophia. After acknowledging that the foursome was fine, Mandana murmured soothingly in Quincy's ear, "Everything is good. You got this, and we've got you."

"Thank you, I—"

Quincy's body stiffened, and Mandana turned her head to follow his gaze toward the door and the couple who had just walked in. The blonde-haired woman was probably shorter than average and looked thin, although her posture and distended belly suggested she was about six or seven months pregnant. The man was significantly taller, with broad shoulders but a sagging build. The woman raised her hand to acknowledge Quincy, and her husband scowled.

The two couples walked toward each other and stopped about an arm's length apart. Quincy opened up, saying, "Hi, this is Mandana. Mandana, this is Stacy and Craig."

"Good to meet you both."

It's not good to meet either of you. She's staring daggers at me, and he looks like he can't decide whether he wants to fuck me or strangle me. Probably both. We're in a public place, and there are cameras everywhere. Just smile and stay cool. And keep Quincy cool.

Stacy responded with, "This is my husband, Craig. Craig, this is Quincy and Mandela."

Mandana slid her arm down Quincy's to grasp his hand and give it a gentle squeeze. "Mandana, not Mandela. Don't worry; I have an unusual name, so it happens to me a lot. You can call me Mandy if it's easier." Mandana kept her tone light and bubbly.

Craig grunted something that might have been generously interpreted as a greeting.

Before Quincy had the chance, Mandana turned and beckoned Ruby forward. She could tell how wary Megan and Tasha were by their stiff postures. Megan rested one hand on Sophia's shoulder, and her other was white-knuckled where it gripped Tasha's. For her part, Ruby looked nervous as she walked forward. Mandana gave Ruby's shoulder a gentle squeeze as she walked by en route to give her mother a hug. She knew Stacy witnessed her gesture, and she read the displeasure on the other woman's face.

That's right, bitch. Ruby belongs here with her father and me, and I want you to know it. She might have come out of you, but you're not her mother. She knows me, trusts me, and I am damn sure I will be a better mother to her. Holy shit, I want to be her mother. Oh, Quincy, you have no idea what you've unleashed.

"Are you pregnant?" Ruby asked.

"I am pregnant. I'm Stacy, and this is Craig. You're going to have a baby brother soon. Isn't that exciting?"

Craig doesn't look excited. He looks possessive, not in a wholesome way. Quincy definitely is not excited—not at all.

"Did you marry Mister Craig because you're pregnant?"

Holy shit, she has no filter, and it's beautiful. I love this girl.

"I married Craig because I love him."

"Why does she talk like a ni—like a Black kid? And what's up with the dykes?"

Craig's first intelligible words, and he spews ignorance and hate. This guy is pure trash.

Quincy responded with a sharp edge of anger in his tone, "Ruby has learned to be polite, which is an important skill. Those people are our friends, Megan and Tasha, along with their daughter, Sophia. Perhaps you should consider learning to be polite…Craig."

Craig grunted angrily, "The fuck did you just say to me?"

Mandana rubbed her thumb along Quincy's hand in slow, soothing circles. In her most pleasant voice, she asked, "Stacy, how long have you and Craig been married?"

The blonde woman gave her a thankful look. Her voice was brittle when she answered, "Almost four months now. We didn't have much time to plan. I wanted to invite Ruby to be the flower girl, but I thought it might be too soon."

Ah, one of those weddings.

"And how did you two lovebirds meet?"

"Um, we were…taking some classes together."

In other words, rehab.

Mandana smiled insincerely. "That's nice. I guess you two must have some common interests."

Well, this extremely awkward silence suggests they have sex and a history of substance abuse in common. And the kid in her belly.

"Mom, how come you didn't marry Daddy when you were pregnant with me?"

"Well, I…"

Quincy came to Stacy's rescue, saying, "Your grandparents really didn't like me a lot back then, and they didn't give us their blessing."

Oh, I bet they love *Craig.*

Stacy nodded. "Yes, your father is right."

"I don't know why. Daddy is so good to me. Why do you want me to live with you?"

Craig rumbled, "Because you should live in a good Christian home and go to a school that teaches you Christian values. You should be surrounded by people who look like you. Not all this mixed crap."

Yep, pure trash.

Mandana squeezed Quincy's hand hard as she ever so sweetly asked, "But doesn't the Bible tell us a daughter is the property of her father? It's right there in Exodus 21. There's more in Genesis and First Corinthians."

Thank you, Tasha, for telling me to study specific Bible passages.

"The Bible also says women should be silent," Craig snarled.

Mandana felt Ruby retreat behind her as she and Craig glared at each other.

Quincy broke the silence, saying, "Yeah, I think we're done here. Ruby got to meet her birth mother finally, and it's definitely time for us to leave."

Ouch, "birth mother." Quincy is really making the point about Stacy's role in Ruby's life.

Stacy's eyes followed Ruby's retreat. Mandana saw defeat on the other woman's face. Quietly, Stacy said, "Thank you for meeting us. We should go."

Mandana felt Quincy's hand leave hers, then return a couple of seconds later, pressing what felt like a business card in her hand. As he did this, he said, "Ruby, why don't you give Miss Stacy a hug."

Mandana used this distraction to glance discreetly at the information card for abused women. Once Ruby finished her hug, Mandana moved in to hug Stacy, who was very surprised. She whispered,

"Check your purse," in Stacy's ear as she slid the card into the purse. Quincy then shook Stacy's hand. No one bothered to say goodbye to Craig. Megan and Tasha had moved right behind them to provide additional support, and Sophia was already hugging Ruby as Stacy walked through the exit. Craig stood there glowering until he awkwardly followed.

I would call him an asshole, but that's an insult to assholes, which actually serve a useful function. I may not like Stacy, but I really hope she uses that card.

Tasha said what they were all thinking. "Let's go home."

Chapter 21
I Melt With You
Modern English

Thirty minutes later, they were back at Megan and Tasha's place. The four adults were sitting at the table with glasses of wine, watching the two girls playing with the cats. Quincy could feel his adrenaline levels slowly coming down, but he still felt agitated.

"Well, I'm calling out of work tonight. There's no way I can tend bar without strangling at least one man tonight."

"Good thinking, Mandana," Tasha agreed.

They subsided back into silence, broken only by Mandana tapping on her phone and the occasional sip of wine.

Mandana put her phone down and said, "All right, done. Tasha, how did you know to tell me I should look at some Bible verses and which ones to look at?"

"I grew up Black in South Carolina. I've read the Bible a couple of times. Also, it's a decent bet that the rehab program Stacy went to was probably a religious program. Put two and two together; I figured she might trot out some kind of Bible passage to justify why Ruby should go with them."

"So, you figured Bible passages about fathers owning daughters would be a good counterargument."

"Exactly."

"Forgive my asking, but aren't you an atheist?"

"I am now, but my parents and brother are all Christians."

"Why aren't you a Christian?"

"Because I read the Bible a couple of times." Tasha laughed before continuing, "You read that passage in Exodus 21 about selling your own daughter as a sex slave. Slavery and misogyny ain't right. Shit like selling daughters made me an atheist." Tasha lovingly took Megan's hand. "Then I started dating women."

"I'm guessing you gave Quincy the card for a women's shelter for the same reason?"

"Pretty much."

"Damn, you are brilliant, Tasha, although I'm not surprised."

"Thanks, Mandana."

It's adorable to see Megan looking at Tasha with such love. I hope Mandana and I look at each other with the same love someday.

"Do you think she will use the card and call the shelter?"

"Sadly, no. What about you, Quincy? What do you think she will do?"

"I agree with Tasha. Probably not. I really hope she does, but I suspect she will stay with a guy who is clearly abusive. I'm pretty sure her parents were abusive, and drugs became her coping mechanism. I feel like Stacy might be one of those people who never escape the cycle of abuse. I hate to say it, and like I said, I hope she calls."

Mandana reached over and took his hand. "I'm sorry, Quincy. Today must have been tough."

He exhaled. "Yeah, it sucked a lot. One thing is for sure: I will never let Ruby near Craig. I saw the hungry look in his eye, and—" Quincy felt a surge of rage. "I'll castrate him before I let him near her."

Mandana nodded vigorously. "I agree with Quincy. It's a good thing you two couldn't hear him. I think castration is far too nice. I saw the same look and could've gutted him on the spot."

I'm glad she saw what I did. It wasn't just my intense dislike of him.

"On that note, I need to go and talk to Ruby."

Quincy stood up and walked over to the girls. "Sophia, can I talk to Ruby for a minute?"

"Yes, Mister Quincy."

Once Sophia went over to her moms, Quincy sat down next to Ruby. "How are you feeling after meeting your mother for the first time, kiddo?"

"I don't know, Daddy. I'm excited to have a brother, but it's weird. Like, I didn't know he even existed before today, so I don't know how I'm supposed to feel. Will I even see him?"

"Well, you can see your brother if you want. I mean, you could even choose to live with him."

I really hope she doesn't want to, especially because I don't like how Craig looked at her. Maybe it's in my head, but he gave off evil vibes.

Ruby shook her head vigorously. "No. He seemed like a very bad man." His daughter shivered. "He scared me."

"Your mom's new husband? I didn't like him, either."

"He gave me goosebumps. I don't ever want to see him again."

Quincy hugged Ruby close. "That makes two of us."

From the depths of the hug, her little voice asked, "Daddy, is Miss Mandana gonna get pregnant with a brother or sister?"

Not gonna lie, I much preferred when she was asking Stacy the hard questions. How do I answer this? Very carefully.

"No, sweetheart. Miss Mandana has decided she doesn't want to have kids of her own."

Ruby's voice quavered, "Does that mean she doesn't want me?"

Quincy hugged her closer. "I think she wants you, little angel. You are already her *azizam*. Miss Mandana doesn't want to get pregnant and had an operation to ensure she can't."

"She can decide that?"

"Yes. You can make the same decision, too, if you want. We will have some long talks about pregnancy and other stuff over the next few years. If you do want a brother or sister, then we could think about adopting."

"No, I'm okay. Sophia is my sister. Now I have one Daddy and three Mommies."

"Well, your mom will be going back to Florida soon."

Ruby giggled at Quincy's thick-headedness. "No, silly! I meant Sophia's Mommies and Miss Mandana."

I really need to have another talk with Mandana.

"Daddy?"

"Yes, sweetheart?"

"Can I spend the night here with Sophia? Today was hard, and we think a sleepover would be the best way to end it."

"We, huh? Let me ask her Moms."

"Thank you, Daddy!"

"All right, I'll go ask them now."

Quincy stood up and walked back to the adults, passing Sophia headed the other direction.

Megan looked at him and said, "Let me guess, Ruby asked you if she could spend the night here with Sophia."

"Yes, apparently, they want to have a sleepover. I think it's a great idea, provided you all don't mind."

"Tasha and I are totally fine with having Ruby here. She had a rough day, and time with Sophia will be good for her."

"Well, I guess I'll have the apartment to myself tonight."

"Perhaps not—" Mandana looked at him coyly. "—maybe you and I could have a sleepover."

Quincy gulped audibly. Megan and Tasha just grinned.

"I do mean a sleepover, Quincy. You aren't putting Quincy Junior inside of any part of me until I see a clean test report."

Tasha decided to chime in with, "Is his tongue allowed?"

"Possibly. Quincy, did your tongue get inside Sara?"

"Only her mouth."

"I'll think about it."

Quincy sat down quickly before his knees gave out.

There goes my blood pressure again.

The four adults chatted about lighter topics for about fifteen minutes before inviting the girls to the table for Settlers of Catan. The six of them played multiple games up until dinner time. Ruby and Sophia wanted grilled cheese sandwiches for dinner and offered to make them for everyone. The adults stood and talked, keeping an unobtrusive eye on the two girls as they made dinner. After dinner, Megan and Tasha shepherded the girls into the living room for a movie, leaving Mandana and Quincy alone.

Staring at their retreating backs, Quincy commented, "They aren't subtle at all."

Mandana chuckled. "Nope."

"When you suggested a sleepover, did you have any thoughts on where?"

"I was thinking about your place."

"Um, fair warning, my place is a mess right now."

"Good."

"Good? Really?"

"Yes. Quincy, I have lived alone for years now. I *want* something messy. I want lived-in. I..."

Quincy hung in suspense as Mandana trailed off. "What?"

"Forget about it."

He decided not to press the matter. "Okay. Do you need to go home to get something to sleep in?"

Mandana's voice dropped into a throaty murmur as she answered, "Not really."

"Oh…"

"Quincy?"

"Yes?"

"Take me home."

They said goodbye to everyone and were ushered out the door to the tune of Megan and Tasha's lecherous giggling. Hand-in-hand, they strolled back to Quincy's apartment. Once inside, Quincy excused himself so he could feed Dolly Purrton. Dolly was incredibly excited because this was the first time she had been fed in her entire life, or at least that's what she was communicating. Quincy was so busy talking with Dolly and tending to her needs that he forgot about Mandana. When he looked up, he couldn't see her. Just her jacket slumped over the couch. Coming out of the kitchen, he saw her vest on the floor. A little beyond the vest was one boot, with its mate further on. As Quincy followed this incredibly erotic trail, he next came upon a tiny bit of fabric in front of his closed bedroom door. Opening the door, he saw Mandana stretched out on his bed wearing stockings. Just stockings.

"You are overdressed," she purred.

"You're definitely right."

Quincy corrected this problem as quickly as his nervous hands allowed.

"Socks, too."

"Oh, right."

"Um, I thought, you know..."

"When do you get your test results back?"

"Initial results are clean, but the full results won't be ready until Monday. Maybe Tuesday."

"Let's hope for a clean result on Monday. You're going to have to wait until then before he—" She pointed at his half-mast erection. "—goes inside me. Until then, we'll have other kinds of fun. Any objections?"

I really regret my night with Sara right now. Tonight, I will make it all about pleasing her.

"I agree to your terms. I do have a clarifying question, though."

"What is it?"

"Have you made a decision regarding my tongue?"

Mandana kept him in suspense. "Possibly. What were you thinking?"

She really seemed to like the silliest innuendos last time, so here goes—

"I hear there is an all-night buffet at the bearded clam bar, and I'd like to try it."

Mandana curled up laughing, kicking her legs in the air, which provided Quincy with an incredible view. "All-night buffet at the bearded clam bar, huh? Yes, get your tongue over here."

Quincy crawled up next to Mandana and kissed her—softly at first but with increasing intensity. Their tongues engaged in vigorous debate as their hands explored. After a while, Quincy pulled back.

"Hey, Mandana. Um. Can we stop for a minute?"

Her expression shifted from lustful to concerned. "Sure, what's up?"

"First, thank you for the sleepover idea. I really appreciate it."

"Uh-huh."

"Second, this...what we were doing just now is something I really enjoy and kinda need after today. And I appreciate you as well."

"Uh-huh."

"What I'm trying to say is I have a ton of emotional stuff going on right now, and while doing all this physical stuff helps, I kinda feel like it is just masking the emotional stuff."

"Me too. Maybe just hold me for a while." Mandana closed the distance between them, settling herself underneath his arm with her head on his shoulder. She pressed her body against his with one leg draped across his legs.

Mandana shivered and clutched him. "Quincy, I saw his eyes when he looked at Ruby. I saw his eyes when he looked at me. There's not a man in there. He's a fucking monster. You can't let her near him. Promise me."

"I saw it, too. I promise you I will always protect her."

There was rage in her voice when she said, "Good. Because you're nicer than me. I will fucking kill him before he ever has a chance to hurt her."

"Are you saying this because you have such a visceral reaction to him or because you care about Ruby?"

Mandana held him tighter. "Both, but mostly the latter. As much as I would love to see a purge of all of the predators and monsters out there, it isn't gonna happen. But any who are a threat to Ruby…for them, I have no mercy."

"Wow, I didn't know you cared for her so deeply."

"Honestly, I don't think I knew until today. Quincy?"

"Yeah?"

"We're going to protect her, no matter what. The engagement, real or not, is happening even if I have to buy my own damn ring. And—" Mandana pulled herself up to kiss him before settling back down. "—Fuck, this is hard to say. You know…the right words and stuff."

Quincy gently stroked her hair. "Can I try?"

"Sure. I'm struggling here."

He chuckled self-deprecatingly. "I'm struggling, too. Mandana, I want to protect Ruby—more than anything in the world. When we started this, I was crystal clear about how I wanted to protect Ruby from you. It was the right decision at the time, but that time has passed." Another self-deprecating chuckle. "The funny part is, along the way, I've discovered my daughter is a lot smarter than me and has manipulated me multiple times to bring us closer together. Ruby likes you. She likes you a lot."

Mandana whispered, "She told me I make you smile."

"She's right. You do make me smile. You also make my brain crash and my heart race. You challenge me and make me think. What I'm getting at is—"

Say the words, Quincy. Stop screwing around and say the damn words.

Mandana placed a finger on his lips. She shifted her body so all Quincy could see was her face just a hand's breadth away from his. Their eyes were locked on each other.

"Hang on. Let me…"

Quincy felt her breasts press against his arm and chest as Mandana reached behind her head and pulled. Her hair cascaded down into a dark, salt-and-pepper curtain framing their faces. Mandana's smile was shy and kind as she said, "Quincy, I love you." Then she kissed him. He felt a rush of joy in his heart. Her kiss was soft and sweet, lingering on the lips before pulling away. Quincy could see the moisture in her eyes.

"Thank you. I love you, too, Mandana."

The tears fell in a soft rain on his cheeks. Their lips met again, soft and gentle, as more tears fell. Quincy held Mandana tight, feeling the waves of emotion sweeping through their bodies. The kiss transitioned from one long kiss to a series of progressively shorter kisses until Mandana moved slightly, her nose resting on Quincy's cheek.

"You said Ruby likes me and has been trying to get us together. Are you sure? Because it would break my heart if you were wrong."

"I talked with her this afternoon. Do you want to know what she told me?"

"Please."

"Ruby told me she has one Daddy and three Mommies. Megan, Tasha, and you, Mandana. You're one of her Mommies."

Mandana wept again. Quincy held her close, gently stroking her back, this time joining Mandana in the waterfall of teardrops. He felt her gently kiss away their commingled tears. Beneath the ebony curtain of Mandana's hair, Quincy could see her tender smile.

"Quincy, earlier when I told you I wanted to come here because I wanted lived-in and messy, there was another thing. I wasn't ready to say it then." Mandana's voice was soft and quiet. "I'm ready to say it now, though. Um. Almost ready."

"It's okay. Take your time. I'm not going anywhere," he murmured soothingly.

"Of course, you aren't going anywhere. You have a naked woman draped all over you."

"An incredibly beautiful, smart, loving, and sexy naked woman."

"Mmmm, don't you have a silver tongue?"

"I'm prepared to make good use of my tongue."

Mandana moaned, "I like the sound of that."

"As much as I like the direction of our flirting, I still want to give you space to finish your thoughts. If you want."

"Damn, you are hot. Sorry, the third thing. I want to spend the night with you. Not just tonight, but many nights."

"What do you mean when you say a lot?" Quincy asked huskily.

In a quiet voice, Mandana answered, "I've been trying not to think about it too much. Honestly, I'm terrified by what I want."

"You don't have to say anymore if you don't want to."

"I know, thank you. I want to, though. *Every night.* I wish I could spend every night with you." She shivered against him. "I'm scared because I want to wake up with you every morning. Wake up, kiss you, roll out of bed, and make Ruby breakfast. I've never wanted such a deep relationship before."

Quincy tenderly rubbed her back. "I can see how permanence could be frightening."

"You aren't worried?"

"I think it's a bit different for me because I've been living with Ruby for the past eight years. I really like the idea of waking up next to you and kissing you. Not a fan of the getting out of bed part, though." Quincy couldn't stop himself from leering at Mandana.

Mandana's peals of laughter reverberated off the walls. "You pig. I'm gonna get you." Using her superior positioning, she immediately started to tickle him. Realizing he was losing, Quincy did the wise thing.

"I surrender, I surrender."

"Hmmm, what should I do to my conquered foe?"

"Is your conquered foe allowed to voice an opinion?"

Mandana sat up and contemplated this thoughtfully.

How am I this lucky? I could watch her for the rest of my life.

"Fine. I will carefully consider your opinion."

"You are graceful in victory, my queen."

"My queen? You may refer to me as your queen from now on."

"Perhaps I should be required to bring your victorious self to orgasm?"

"Oh, you naughty peasant. Yes, you are commanded to bring your queen to orgasm. With. Your. Tongue." Mandana fell backward, legs splayed wide. "The all-you-can-eat bearded clam bar is open for dining."

"I feel like I mentioned before how I'm not very good at this."

"Don't worry, lover. Just follow my directions. Come over here and get comfortable. Gaze upon the promised land. Here in the North is the clitoris and the clitoral hood. This is my pleasure palace. Further South is the urethra, the pee hole. If you aren't willing to put your mouth on mine, then don't expect me to put my mouth on yours."

"Makes sense to me."

"Plus, more nerve endings around there. Further South, we reach the vaginal opening or your promised land. Give me your finger." Quincy watched as she guided him inside. He felt her adjust his finger to the upper side of her vagina. "Feel this rough patch? That's the G-spot. You need to pay attention to it. Finally, around the whole thing is my labia. The lips. Basically, you have this lovely little playground in which to make me very, very happy."

"Got it."

"Good, now get your mouth down by the tops of my stockings and tease me with your lips and tongue."

Oh, teacher, I plan to get an A-plus tonight. Or maybe it's an O-plus.

"Your nose and chin can help, too. That's enough teasing for now. I want you to kiss me all over. Just little kisses. Start at the clit and go down the lips and back up. Good boy. This is a good thing to do when your tongue gets tired. Mmmm, you're doing so well, Quincy," she purred.

This is amazing. She's really wet.

"Next, I want you to give my lips some deeper kisses, get your head in there and move your mouth up and down, nibbling and sucking. Fuck, you're doing so well. All right, back to the clit. Circle it with your tongue. Get under it with your tongue. Circle around the hood. *Oh*, yes. Can you go back to those kisses? I need a break before we get fingers involved."

"Am I doing a good job?"

"You're doing great, I—"

Oh, shit. She's crying. Why is she crying? I can't be that bad, right?

Quincy crawled up beside Mandana and cradled her head to his chest as she sobbed. He made soothing noises and gently stroked her hair and skin. Slowly, Mandana went from bawling to quiet weeping and, finally, a soft whimper. Quincy tenderly asked, "Do you want to tell me what's wrong?"

"I'm sorry, Quincy. You were making me feel so good, and I just got overwhelmed. I'm barking orders at you like a drill sergeant while you're eating me out, and I felt like such a bitch."

"No, you're not a bitch. Mandana. It was actually very helpful for me. I've never felt adequate about my oral skills, so having you tell me what to do is great."

"You're not mad at me?"

"Of course not."

"It's just—both times we've been together, I've been so demanding and selfish. I'm really sorry. I—"

He squeezed Mandana tighter in his arms. "What is it?"

"Quincy, please don't leave me."

"I'm not going anywhere. I promise. If it's something too painful to talk about, then you don't have to. I'm happy to just hold you."

"You're very considerate and sweet. I'm sorry I'm such a mess."

"We are all messy in our own ways."

"Remember when I told you I needed clitoral stimulation to orgasm?"

"I remember."

"It took me years to realize." Another soft sob. "Is it okay if I tell you this?"

"Mandana, I told you I was high as a kite when I got Stacy pregnant, and you're still here. I think if you can handle my dirty laundry, then I can handle this."

"Thank you. I lost my virginity in high school, and it was awful. I had sex a few more times in high school, and it was...not great. Sometimes, I enjoyed it a little, but it was never good. In college, I experimented with a couple of women. The first time I ever orgasmed during sex was with a woman. Unfortunately for me, I'm attracted to women, but I've never wanted to date a woman seriously. Eventually, after college, I finally figured out the clitoral stimulation thing."

"I'm so sorry. Sex gets built up as this great thing, but you mostly weren't able to enjoy it."

"Exactly. And for the most part, guys didn't seem to care, or even if they did, they just assumed they needed to fuck harder, which didn't help. So, I just faked it. They got to feel better about themselves, and I just felt worse."

Quincy squeezed her tight. "I'm sorry you had such miserable experiences."

"It was. So once I figured it out, I decided I wasn't just going to lie there for someone else's pleasure anymore. I became more vocal and demanding because I wanted pleasure, too."

He nodded. "Seems fair."

"Thank you for saying so because everyone else just ran off. Maybe they stayed for one night, but no more. After a while, I just stopped trying. I haven't been with anyone in almost six years."

Quincy was stunned. "Wow. Six years is a long time. I'm so sorry." He paused and ran his fingertips in circles on her skin. "Mandana, I want you to know I'm not abandoning you. I will be here now. I'll be here in the morning. And I'll be here the next morning. And every morning going forward."

She started crying again, tears falling on his chest. He just held her, letting her emotions run their course.

I've always seen her as such a badass, but I never realized just how lonely that was for her. Having Ruby means I'm never truly alone, but I've still been lonely as well, although I'm not sure I thought about it a lot. Now, I don't feel lonely anymore. Instead, I feel loved. Like there was a Mandana-sized hole in my life I didn't even know was there.

"Mandana? I just realized something we didn't discuss earlier."

"What?"

"You said this engagement was happening to protect Ruby, regardless of whether it is real." She nodded before he continued. "I want it to be real. Before you say anything, I need to finish. I don't want to marry you because I want to protect Ruby. I want to marry you because you are amazing and wonderful, and I love you. I'll sign whatever prenup you want me to sign."

She sounded surprised. "Are you proposing to me? For real? Like this?"

"Mandana Davani, will you marry me?"

"Abso-fucking-lutely yes," Mandana gushed. "But we are never, and I mean *never*, telling anyone you proposed to me while we were naked in bed with me bawling my eyes out on your surprisingly comfortable chest."

"I can accept your terms," Quincy smiled at her. "We'll make up a story."

"Oh, maybe we can do it again, you know, publicly. Do the whole cheesy romance movie proposal in a restaurant or on a cliff or something." Mandana giggled.

"I could have Ruby hand you a box with the ring while I got down on one knee, then you would turn around, see me kneeling there, and you would act all surprised. Then I can make a little speech about making me the happiest man alive, which is totally true already. You'll say 'Yes,' and people will clap, and I'll put the ring on your finger. For the grand finale, the three of us will hug, and there won't be a dry eye in sight."

"I'm impressed, Quincy. Well done."

"I'll make sure you are very well done afterward," he said lewdly.

"Oh, my. Not to break the mood or anything, but—"

"What is it?"

"I'm really out of the mood right now. Do you mind if I take off these stockings and just fall asleep in your arms?"

"Do you want me to get you something to sleep in?"

Quincy waited as Mandana pondered her answer. "Honestly, I would like to sleep naked with you. Being naked with you like this makes me feel vulnerable but also safe. Am I making sense?"

"You are. I've never intentionally slept naked with someone before. I'm feeling the same thing. Like there are no secrets."

"I haven't, either. Speaking of secrets—" Mandana shyly bit her lower lip, which Quincy found incredibly attractive. "—ever since I started doing nude yoga, I've spent most of my time at home completely naked. I really like it." She looked him in the eye and asked accusingly, "Did your dick just twitch?"

"What?" Quincy responded defensively. "It's not my fault you put an image of you lounging around naked in my head. Speaking of, how does being naked make you feel?"

"Free. Empowered. Sexy."

"I bet. Any other secrets I should know?"

"No. You?"

"None I can think of. I will warn you to keep your feet covered because Dolly Purrton will attack your toes in the night."

"Good to know."

As the two of them were lying in bed cuddling, they were interrupted by an incoming message on Quincy's phone. "Sorry, I need to check to see if it's about Ruby."

"Go right ahead."

Quincy fished his phone out of his discarded pants. Standing there completely naked, he unlocked his phone. There was one new message for him. "That's weird."

"What's weird? Who is it from?"

Quincy sat down on the edge of the bed and felt Mandana crawl up behind him with her chin on his shoulder. "It's from Sara." He felt her body stiffen. "She's asking me if I'm up. What does she mean?"

"You don't know?"

Quincy tapped out a quick response.

"What did you just tell her?"

"I said I'm in bed right now. *Oh*, she just asked me if I wanted some company."

Mandana's voice gained a hint of steel. "Quincy, are you sure you have no more secrets?"

"Yes, see. Here's my text history. I texted Sara a couple of times to set up our date, and then nothing until tonight."

She snickered at him. "You silly man. A text asking 'You up?' is code asking if you want sex, and you just told her you want to."

"I did?"

"May I?" Mandana held out her hand.

"Um, you're going to be nice, right?"

"I promise."

"All right." Quincy handed Mandana the phone. "What did you just type?"

"Oh, I asked her if she remembered the bartender from your date. Interestingly, Sara remembers me and says I'm smoking hot. Maybe I don't dislike this girl so much."

"She's right, you are incredibly hot."

"Now I told her you and I are dating, and I'm keeping your bed warm."

"My bed has been cold and lonely," he responded with faux sorrow.

"Wow. Cheeky girl. She says three's company if you think you can handle two women at once. Oh, another text. Sara says when you need a break, she is happy to play with just me."

Quincy rushed to reassure her. "You are all I need, Mandana."

Mandana cocked an eyebrow at him. "You're turning down a threesome with me and this nubile minx?"

"Even if I wasn't already getting tested because of my prior...liaison with Sara, you're still all I need."

"What if *I* wanted to have a threesome with us and Sara?"

"Huh. *Really?*" He didn't bother to hide his confusion. "I thought you didn't like her."

"Sara is assertive, confident, and sexy. I like those qualities, so maybe she's growing on me. The best sex of my life so far has been with women, and she's not interested in a relationship with you—so I might entertain this idea." Mandana paused and looked Quincy straight in the eyes. "You also didn't answer my question about whether you would do this if I wanted to have a threesome with Sara."

Damn. I was hoping she would miss my silence. Mandana is texting again.

"What are you saying now?" Quincy asked, sounding worried.

"I didn't want to leave the poor girl hanging while we talked, so I said you and I were discussing it. I also said I made you get tested before we had sex, and we're awaiting the results." Mandana stared at him. "You're still not answering my question."

"Okay, here goes. If you would like us to have a threesome with Sara, then I would consider it; however, I would want the two of us to talk about it within the context of our relationship first. Also, I would want all three of us to talk about it together before anything happens. So, definitely not tonight. More importantly, I would like our first time together to be just us."

"Damn, Quincy. Solid answer. And you're right. Our first time should be just the two of us. Oh, here we go. Sara says that while she figured in the moment you were a safe bet, she got herself tested anyway, just in case. And she sent pictures of the results."

"What does it say?"

"Nothing to worry about."

"So..."

"We don't have to wait on your results."

"Fuck yes," Quincy cheered. He quickly added soberly, "But not right now because you aren't in the mood. Also, I don't want to fuck you. I want to make love to you."

"You can make love to me tomorrow. And then fuck me silly. Okay, I need to text Sara back. Um. Let's say, 'Sara, thank you for your offer. Mandana and I need to talk and ensure we are secure in our relationship before we consider adding someone else.' Sounds good?"

"I like it."

"Whoa, fast response. Sara says that is beautiful, followed by heart emojis, eggplant emojis, and multiple X's and O's."

"Aw, very nice. Now, can we put my phone back and cuddle ourselves to sleep?"

Chapter 22

Love Me Like You Do

Ellie Goulding

There was something hard pressed against Mandana's butt, and her back was warm and slicked with sweat. As the fog of sleep lifted, the memories of the previous night came rushing back. Quincy's warm breath was in her hair, and his gentle snores were in her ears. One of his arms was draped comfortably across her, hand resting against her underboob. She felt tears welling in her eyes as she remembered their confessions of love and his hurried proposal.

Will he still feel the same in the light of day? More importantly, will he still feel the same when I'm wearing clothes again? Is this fear speaking, making me question Quincy? The man turned down a threesome because he wanted me. That's gotta mean something.

Next question: Did I mean those things I said last night? Yesterday was an emotional roller coaster. I can't be blamed if I was swept away, right? I definitely fear talking. I knew before yesterday I was falling for him; I just didn't want to admit it. Admitting I love Quincy and care for his daughter means letting someone in. It means I'm vulnerable.

I slept naked in a man's bed. It doesn't get much more vulnerable. Especially since he is naked, too, how many men would have agreed to spend the night like this without sex, without any release? How many would have called me a cocktease, or, worse, taken me in my sleep? If I still believed in Ahura Mazda, then I would pray Quincy still feels the same.

Mandana gently extricated herself from Quincy's somnolent embrace and quietly padded to the bathroom. Emerging a few minutes later, she stopped, shyly covering herself from Quincy's now open eyes.

Recognizing her reticence, Quincy quickly shut his eyes. "I'm sorry, Mandana. I didn't mean to stare."

"Quincy, everything we said last night. It wasn't some fit of madness, was it? In the harsh light of day, do you still mean it?"

"Every word, Mandana. I meant it then, I mean it now, I will mean it forever." His eyes remained firmly shut.

"Look at me, please." Mandana pulled her arms to her hips and cocked a leg in a power pose. A pose that also left her completely exposed.

Quincy opened his eyes and turned toward her. She could see his eyes drinking in her body like a desert wanderer at an oasis. There was hunger in those eyes, but beyond the longing, there was love and tenderness. A tent was forming in the middle of the bed.

"Mmmm, it looks like someone is happy to see me," Mandana growled lasciviously. Like the Persian lioness she was, she stalked toward the bed, watching Quincy's eyes grow to saucer size. Lifting the covers, she slid underneath, molding herself to his body.

"Quincy, I'm sorry about my moment of doubt. Vulnerability is hard for me. Thank you for being understanding."

"Of course, Mandana. I would be lying if I said I didn't also wonder if you would feel the same in the morning."

"Thank you. Hmmm, it appears vulnerability isn't the only thing hard for me this morning. Just to confirm, do you still want to make love to me this morning?"

"I want to make love to you *every* morning, Mandana."

"Thanks, just wanted to be sure we both want this." Taking hold of Quincy's cock, Mandana stroked him slowly while she brought her lips to his. She felt him roll over on his side to face her, his hands stroking her breasts, abdomen, and ass. They moaned as their tongues cavorted, passions escalating quickly.

Mandana pushed Quincy onto his back while rising up, ensuring their mouths stayed locked. She removed her hand from his turgid member, confirming she was indeed as wet as she thought. Mandana threw one leg over Quincy, straddling him and positioning him in the center of her labia. They both groaned around their tongues as she slowly engulfed his cock. His hands caressed her nipples as she gently rocked up and down, sinking deeper each time.

Once she reached the base of his shaft, Mandana held still, enjoying the pleasant feeling. For the first time in her life, she felt fully connected to a man, physically and emotionally. Quincy held still, allowing her to savor this feeling for as long as she wished. She gave him a squeeze with her pelvic floor muscles, then started slowly riding him.

After a few minutes, Quincy frantically broke their kiss. "Mandana, I'm sorry, but I'm about to—"

"Shhh, it's okay, Quincy. I want you to cum for me." Mandana leaned down to sigh in his ear. "I want you to cum inside me." She felt a series of warm splashes against her cervix as Quincy cried out.

Lying down on top of him, Mandana murmured. "You did so good, Quincy. So good."

"But, I didn't—"

"That's what round two is for. You're *going* to give me round two, aren't you?"

"I might need a couple of minutes."

Mandana nibbled on his ear as he softened inside of her. She kept him there as she moved her lips down his jawline to his other ear. Quincy lolled wearily as she continued her gentle ministrations.

After a while, Quincy suddenly roused in a burst of energy. Mandana groaned as he gripped her hair and firmly brought her lips back to his. She smiled around his tongue as she felt him stiffen inside of her.

Round two, here we go.

Once she felt he was sufficiently hard, Mandana resumed riding Quincy, pulling back for better leverage. The sensations inside of her were exquisite but not enough to get where she wanted to go. Mandana took one of Quincy's hands and brought his fingers to her clit. Immediately realizing his task, Quincy set to work.

"Good boy. Just what I need." *He looks good, lying there all sweaty. He's my man. Mine, now and forever. Holy shit, he's a fast learner.*

Mandana increased her pace until she felt an oncoming wave. Not a wave. A tsunami. She ground down onto him as her orgasm exploded, followed almost immediately by a second, then a third.

"Okay, I might be too sensitive right now. Let me just ride you while I recover a bit."

Quincy nodded wordlessly, moving both hands to her heaving breasts. Mandana reached down to grab the hand which had recently been pleasuring her and brought it to her lips. She watched Quincy's eyes pop as she licked herself off of his fingers.

I love watching his expressions.

Mandana kept up the pace, working his cock like a cowgirl at a rodeo. When her clit cooled down, she brought his fingers back down. The timing was perfect as between orgasms four and five; she saw Quincy's eyes roll back as he dumped a second load inside of her.

She slowly collapsed next to him, finally uncoupling. They lay panting next to each other, their bodies drenched in sweat.

"I know I said it before, under different circumstances, but I want to say it again. I love you, Mandana."

"I love you, too, Quincy. I want you to know something."

"What, my love?"

"I have never cum like that before."

Quincy sighed dreamily, "Cool."

Normally, I would get offended by his response, but I might have broken his brain again.

Mandana was drifting back toward sleep when she heard a buzzing. "Quincy, I think that's your phone."

"Who is calling at this—oh, look at the time." Quincy picked up the phone. "Hey, Megan. Yes, you can bring the girls over this morning. Um, I might need about forty-five minutes."

"We might need about forty-five minutes. And tell Megan I won't make it to nude yoga this morning. You fucked me too good," Mandana commented dreamily.

"Um, she heard you. She says congratulations. Oh, Tasha says congratulations as well."

"Awesome. Tell them we're getting married."

Why did I just say that? Megan definitely caught it because I could hear her shriek. I think Quincy broke my brain. Five orgasms, right? Mmmm, broken brain.

"Yeah, we'll be ready then, I hope," Quincy said, finishing off the conversation with Megan, which finally registered in Mandana's foggy brain.

It took some effort, but forty-five minutes later, Mandana greeted the girls at the door wearing one of Quincy's old T-shirts and some of his drawstring gym shorts. Megan and Tasha leered at her over the girls' heads.

Once the girls raced over to the couch, Megan asked, "Good night?"

"What happened to the 'no sex until tested' rule?" Tasha queried.

"Long story, but a fun one."

Tasha scowled seriously. "Quincy and I have a PTA fundraiser planning session at noon with Mary. Please help him get ready."

"I will, I promise."

Megan added, "I can pick up the girls after yoga so you can go home."

"It's okay if they stay here. I need some practice if I'm going to be Ruby's stepmom."

"You got it bad, girl. Do you know where the first aid kit is, or food?"

"Uhhh."

Megan nodded maternally. "We'll bring the girls over to our place after yoga, and you can come, too. We'll watch the girls together, and I'll give you the rundown for when you do watch the girls by yourself."

"Thanks, Megan. Yesterday, Ruby told Quincy she felt like she had three mothers: the two of you and me. I want to live up to her faith in me." Mandana was immediately drawn into a group hug as the other two women murmured words of appreciation and support.

She smiled when Tasha said, "I'm still learning, too. I'm excited to go on this journey together with you. We're going to be the best stepmoms ever."

Megan and Tasha left for yoga, and Mandana went over to the girls to see if they needed anything. She shooed Quincy off to get cleaned up while she kept an eye on them. Watching Ruby and Sophia wasn't difficult as they were both reading and chatting while petting a blissfully happy Dolly Purrton.

When Quincy was done getting ready, he asked, "Do you want to change out of my old clothes or anything?"

Mandana patted him on the cheek affectionately. "Sweetie, it's cute you think these are still your clothes. I'm very comfortable as is, and I really don't want to put on yesterday's clothes. Do you mind if I talk to Ruby about us, or would you like to speak with her together?"

There's his thinking face. I like how he usually takes the time to consider what to say and tries to find the best possible words.

"I think we really do need to talk with her together at some point, but I am okay with you talking with her on your own about us. I trust you."

Damn, he's sexy when he's thoughtful.

"Thank you, *Eshgham.* Maybe you can sit with Sophia while I talk with Ruby."

"*Eshgham?*"

"It translates into, 'my love.'"

Quincy smiled in response.

Mandana took a seat at the table and was pleasantly surprised when Ruby suggested they sit on the floor together instead. They sat down, and Ruby asked, "Did you have a nice sleepover with Daddy?"

Wow. That was not the question I wanted to hear, especially asked so innocently.

"We did have a nice sleepover. Your father and I had a chance to really talk and express ourselves. Are you okay with your father and me having a sleepover?"

"Yes, Miss Mandana. What did you and Daddy talk about?"

"We talked about how we feel about each other and our relationship. I would like to talk with you a bit about us. Is that okay with you?"

"Do you like me, Miss Mandana?"

"You get right to the point, don't you?" Mandana asked rhetorically. Smiling sweetly, she continued, "I really like you, Ruby. You are very smart and observant. You're also sweet and really good to your father. I want to be honest with you. Many years ago, I decided I didn't want to be a mom. It was a decision that required a great deal of thought. Then something happened. I met you and your Dad. I can never be your actual mom, but I really want to be a part of your life."

Ruby shuffled over and gave Mandana a big hug. "Miss Mandana, you always talk to me like I'm a big girl and not a little kid. You make Daddy really happy. He always smiles when he thinks of you. I like the dopey faces he makes when you aren't looking."

He does, does he? Good to know.

"I see you make goo-goo eyes at him, too."

I do?

"You're smart and kind and really pretty. I like how you make time for me. And you love Daddy a lot. I would like you to be my mommy." Ruby looked at her curiously. "Miss Mandana, why are you crying?"

Mandana sniffled and wiped at her tears. "Because I'm really happy, *Azizam*. Sometime soon, the three of us need to sit down and talk about our future. In the meantime, do you mind if I have more sleepovers?"

"You mean like tonight? Would you and my Dad walk me to school tomorrow?"

"I would love to, *Khoshgelam*. Which means 'my pretty one' in Farsi."

"Will you teach me Farsi?"

"Of course, *Azizam*."

"I love you, Miss Mandana."

"I love you, too, Ruby."

And I will be worthy of your love, Azizam.

Chapter 23
Beautiful Day
U2

Megan and Tasha took the girls to their place after yoga, briefly leaving Mandana and Quincy alone. Mandana changed back into her clothing from the day before but carefully kept what she borrowed from Quincy separated from the rest of his clothing.

"Quincy, there's something else we need to talk about," Mandana said playfully.

"What is it?"

"You're going to have to tell me what clothes of yours are off-limits because I'll probably steal more of your shirts."

"Can I ask why?"

"They're comfortable, they smell like you, and wearing one of your shirts makes me feel closer to you. It's like wearing a hug."

Quincy shot her a sultry look. "You're also really sexy wearing one of my shirts."

Mandana's eyes twinkled as she laughed. "Because my ass is hanging out. Speaking of, if I wear my really stupid stilettos, would it bother you that I would be taller?"

"No, I wouldn't mind at all."

"Good. All right, I'm going to go home to get clothes and stuff. Ruby told me she wants us to walk her to school tomorrow morning."

"Well, that just got my blood pumping. It sounds like Ruby is okay with another sleepover. I'd like it if you spent the night here. The implications are very domestic."

She smiled shyly. "I *want* to be domestic with you. Is that okay?"

He hugged her. "Definitely."

"Ruby asked if we had a good sleepover last night. I told her we did, and we had a chance to talk about a lot of important things. Just in case you're about to ask, I did *not* mention the sex."

"That's good. I didn't think you would. Anything else I should know?"

I recognize her pause. That's Mandana's "I have something signific-icant to say, but I'm struggling with the words" pause. I just need to give her space and she'll get there.

"I made a promise to myself that I will be the best mother I can be to Ruby."

"Wow. Thank you for telling me. I will do whatever I can to support you."

Mandana nodded and squeezed him tight. She then released him and fled, rocketing out the door.

I think I might have touched a nerve, hopefully in a good way. I have to hope it's not bad because I need to meet Tasha and Mary soon. Should I text her? I'll just give her some space.

Mandana: *Sorry. It's not you, it's me.*

I just got overwhelmed.

I love you, and I'll see you soon.

Quincy: *Thank you.*

The meeting with Mary and Tasha was lengthy but productive. They all agreed that the fundraiser was coming along nicely. Mary commented after the main business concluded, "It's too bad you and Sara didn't hit it off. You're a good catch; she could use a man like you."

It's a good thing Mary can't see Tasha's face right now because she looks like she's about to crack up.

"I have a friend I think would be perfect for you. Let me give you her number."

"Mary, I gotta stop you right there. Thank you very much. Sara was a charming young woman, and I was happy to meet her, but I have a girlfriend."

"You do? That's great, Quincy. Can I see a picture of her?"

Shit. It's all happened so fast; we don't even have any...yes, yes, we do.

Quincy dug into his photo gallery and pulled up the fake girlfriend kiss photo Mandana had made with him weeks ago. He showed Mary the picture. "She is beautiful, Quincy. Congratulations. Okay, then, I will see you two soon. Ta!"

As they walked back to Tasha's place, Quincy waited for the inevitable. "So, were you happy to meet Sara or put your meat in her?" Tasha snickered.

Quincy sighed. "Let me guess, you also want to comment about how Sara used a man like me."

Tasha beamed. "You guessed my next line."

"You really enjoy teasing me, don't you?"

"It is fun." Tasha cackled gleefully.

"Did I mention how Sara texted me last night while I was in bed with Mandana?"

"She didn't..."

"Oh, she did. She even offered to come over for a threesome."

"You're lying."

"I swear I'm telling the truth."

"What did you say?"

"No, of course."

"What did Mandana say?"

"That she would think about it some other time."

Tasha's eyes went wide as saucers. "What? Really? She's so hot. I mean, don't mess up a great thing for a threesome, but still...wait, do you think she actually would?"

"I'm not sure. It was a strange moment."

"I bet."

"Weirdly, I felt closer to Mandana afterward. Talking about it strengthened our bond."

"That does sound weird. Anyway, no talk of threesomes around the girls."

Quincy just gave her a look, which expressed everything he needed to say.

Mandana had been there for a while and was talking with Megan when they entered. Everyone hugged, including the girls who bounced up from playing a game. The adults chatted while the girls finished their game, and then Mandana, Quincy, and Ruby headed out. Mandana promised to meet them at the apartment but wanted to do some shopping first. They weren't home long before she arrived, laden with groceries.

"What's in the bags?"

"We're having chicken cordon bleu tonight, and you and Ruby are going to help me fix a nice family dinner."

"Sounds fancy. Are you trying to broaden my horizons?"

"I am, *Delbar*. Which means, 'the one who stole my heart.'"

"Thank you, *Eshgham*."

"Quincy, you remembered," Mandana gushed. She dropped the groceries on the table, threw her arms around his neck, and kissed him passionately.

I'm going to need to learn Farsi if this is the reaction I get.

The trio worked on dinner as a family, with Mandana guiding Quincy and Ruby through the process of fixing cordon bleu. Served with flavorful Persian rice and fresh vegetables, the meal was wonderful. Quincy felt relaxed and satisfied, at least until Ruby asked a question.

"Daddy, are you going to marry Miss Mandana?"

Is she practicing to be a journalist? Always the hard questions.

"Sweetheart, Miss Mandana and I talked about marriage last night—"

"During your sleepover."

"Yes, during our sleepover. We talked about getting married, and we would like to, but we need your approval."

"Why do I need to say 'yes'?"

Mandana answered for him, "Because you and your dad have a special bond. You two will always have your bond, and nothing will change that. Your bond means you have just as much of a voice in who becomes part of this family. So, if you say 'No,' then your dad and I won't get married."

"What if I say, 'Yes'?"

"Then we will."

"Will I have to call you Mom?"

"Only if you want to. You should call me whatever you feel comfortable calling me."

"What is it in Farsi?"

"Mom? Well, the formal word for mother is *madar*. For something like mom or mommy, it would be *maman*."

"Yes, *Maman*. You can marry Daddy."

Quincy felt his heart melt. He and Mandana both hugged Ruby, showering her with kisses before looking at each other and exchanging quiet words of love. Ruby eventually squirmed out to go read her book with Dolly Purrton. Quincy went to wash the dishes while Mandana disappeared into the bedroom. A few minutes later, she emerged in silk pajama pants and his favorite Def Leppard t-shirt to sit with a book next to Ruby and Dolly.

Look at them just sitting together comfortably. The girl I have loved for all eight years of her life and the woman I fell in love with. I can't imagine a life without either or both of them. This is the family I want.

After the dishes were done, Quincy sat on the floor in front of the couch with his book and felt Mandana start idly twirling her fingers in his hair. This position didn't do his back any favors, but any stiffness was a worthwhile trade for the fullness in his heart. Fortunately for Quincy's back, Ruby had to go to bed soon. Mandana assisted in putting her to bed. Once Ruby was tucked in and the three of them had read to each other from her book, the two adults retreated to his...their bedroom.

Quincy decided that maybe changing the sheets would be a good idea after the morning's exertions, a task he was finishing as Mandana emerged from the bathroom wearing only his Def Leppard shirt.

Holy shit. She is smoking hot. Her ass is definitely hanging out.

Mandana glided up to him, sliding her arms around his neck. She kissed him softly. Quincy's hands slid down her back to her bare ass, which he squeezed enthusiastically.

"Down, boy. I am not having hot and noisy sex in earshot of Ruby."

"Hot and quiet sex?" Quincy asked hopefully.

"*Eshgham*, I don't think I can be quiet with you. I promise that the next time it is Tasha's turn to watch the girls, we will get very loud and *very* sweaty. Tonight, I just want to sleep naked with you. Feeling your skin on mine comforts me."

He kissed her affectionately. "I'd like that. I feel the same way."

"Do you need me to take care of your problem...down there?"

"No, thank you. He needs to learn how to behave around a lady."

"I'm your lady. By the way, you didn't want this shirt back, did you?"

"Nope. It looks better on you."

With a saucy wink, Mandana said, "I bet it looks even better on the floor." She pulled off the shirt and slid into the bed.

In the morning, they reluctantly got up and got dressed. Once all three were ready, they set off for school with Ruby between Mandana and Quincy, holding both of their hands. Tasha gave them a knowing look as she dropped off Sophia. The three adults chatted for a few minutes before going their separate ways. Quincy took some time during the day to bring Maria up to speed on the meeting with Stacy and Craig. He made sure to describe the predatory vibes he and Mandana sensed from Craig. Maria was particularly interested in his description of Ruby's impressions. She thanked him and assured him she would handle things.

Quincy went back to work until he had to pick up the girls from school. He was pleased when Mandana texted to inform him she had rearranged her schedule so she could be at the school with him. They walked the girls back to their place and spent a quiet afternoon reading and playing board games. Once Sophia left, they enjoyed another family dinner and evening together.

Afterword

Mandana stayed over that night, and the next, and the night after that. Eventually, it became clear that her apartment was superfluous. After a serious discussion between the three of them, they went shopping for a ring. Quincy insisted on something elaborate, but Mandana refused. In the end, he bought her a ruby set in a simple gold band, just as she wanted.

The Purrsian Paradise opened up that Spring, which took a lot of Mandana's time. She made sure to have a soft opening with Megan, Quincy, Ruby, Sophia, and Tasha as the first guests. Ruby was delighted that there was a Kitten Korner for kids, which was her idea.

Maria informed Quincy that a private investigator she hired had uncovered a long history of violence and abuse in Craig's past. Armed with this information, Maria ensured Quincy retained full custody of Ruby. Quincy made sure Stacy's parents knew about

Craig, and they adopted Ruby's half-brother when she started using again.

True to his word, Quincy arranged a dream proposal at the picturesque Multnomah Falls, where Ruby delivered a box with a ring to Mandana as he knelt behind her on the damp bridge facing the falls. Mandana turned around, and he asked her to make him the happiest man in the world. Tasha captured the proposal on video while Megan and Sophia held her close. There wasn't a dry eye between any of them.

As Spring turned toward Summer, Mandana and Quincy were the witnesses for Megan and Tasha's wedding. Ruby and Sophia were the flower girls and ring bearers.

Acknowledgements

Thank you to my wife for her support. I could probably manage on my own, but having a caring and supportive partner is so much better. Your support is greatly appreciated.

I'd also like to thank our cats, Merlin, Lady Starlight, and our dearly departed Francesca. A purring cat makes everything better.

Special thanks to my good friend, Steve Davala, who started me on the journey of writing. Your push made a world of difference in my life, and here I am with a *third* self-published novel.

To Katherine Morgan, thank you for your support and encouragement. I'm so excited for your new store: Grand Gesture Books, Oregon's first romance-specific bookstore. I know it will be *incredible,* and I hope it becomes the home-away-from-home for Pacific Northwest romance authors and readers.

Thank you to independent authors and bookstores everywhere! Shop local and independent whenever you can. A special shout out to my independent sci-fi/fantasy writer's community here in Portland and our meet-ups at the Rose City Coffee Co. Another *huge* thank you to my independent author (and romance-specific author) communities on Instagram.

Finally, thank you to the Rose City Rollers community for their continued support.

Chris Walters is a romance author living in Portland, Oregon with his wife and two cats. When not reading, writing, or working, he is an announcer for the Rose City Rollers. He self-published his first novel, No One Like You in June 2024.